LOTUS EFFECT

TRISHA WOLFE

Lock Key Press

Blue,

If I Could Turn Back Time

There is the mud, and there is the lotus that grows out of the mud.

~Thich Nhat Hanh

PROLOGUE
REBIRTH

LAKIN

I remember the way the water rippled from above. The silver light of the moon cast the waves in shimmering motion, as if staring at a theater screen, the movie reel jammed. The projection lamp melting the film.

A life paused, halted. The fabric of time rippling around the seams.

Later, a neurologist would tell me my nervous system was shutting down. My mind, deprived of oxygen, caused bursts of light to flicker across my vision, like one experiences right at the moment of death.

There was no moon that night.

There was only the lake, the vegetation, and my body.

And him.

Through rapidly firing synapses, as the Grim Reaper gripped my soul, I glimpsed his dark silhouette amid the shimmering waves. He drove a hand through the water surface and pulled me from the murky depth.

A phantom. A figment of my imagination.

There was no man.

Only the lotus flowers floating above, their stalks tangling my hair and limbs at the bottom of the lake.

There was only my death.

❧ I ❧

BOOK OF CHELSEA

LAKIN: THEN

I dreamed of my death before it happened.

Between cramming for final exams and packing for spring break, I'd get momentary glimpses. Fleeting wisps, broken fragments of the dream that felt so surreal. I'd shove the abstract images away just as quickly as they came.

It was only a dream.

Then one day, when our Louis Vuitton bags were parked near the mahogany door, my passport in hand—because I just knew I'd forget it otherwise—it happened.

I died.

Right there in the entryway of the beautiful Spanish colonial.

I still remember the sickening acid roiling my stomach. The noxious taste in my mouth as oily vomit clawed up my throat.

I couldn't stop looking at her hair. Like an angel's, her

platinum-blond locks were spun like white gold, wrapping her tan shoulders in a sun-kissed halo around her perfect figure.

"I'm pregnant."

Two words imploded my world. Two little words that, when strung together, changed the course of my life.

I could only stare at her. *I'd dreamt this…*

"I just thought you should know." She crossed her arms, pushing her ample cleavage near her slim throat.

That night, during the fight that would lead to my meltdown, I would unleash every venomous slur and purge every question from my mouth that I should've raised there, but right then, I could only stare vacantly, the earth beneath my Guess wedges shifting me off kilter.

I watched her walk away, down the driveway, her hips swaying.

A sense of déjà vu snatched me. The edges of the dream bleeding in through my stupor.

I knew this was going to happen.

It wasn't a prophecy, of course. Maybe a self-fulfilling one in a sense. The subconscious tickling the conscious, planting hints. Trying its damndest to reveal the truth that our waking minds are too stubborn to accept.

Drew, my psych professor, the only man I had ever loved, had gotten one of his students pregnant.

I crumpled to the marble foyer.

I'd never felt so close to death as I did in that moment. Wanting the world to open up and swallow me—to end my humiliation and misery.

I should've known. I heard it all the time…

Be careful what you wish for.

❧ 2 ❧

IN HER WAKE

LAKIN: NOW

Ｎew chapter:
It's said the lotus represents purity. In Buddhism, the lotus flower is revered, its value to the human condition a staple in many proverbs and metaphors. Gautama Buddha often spoke of how the lotus came from the muddy sludge, and rose above to spring through the water surface unsoiled.

Botanist and lotus expert Thomas Ryker explains the lotus effect more scientifically, describing the self-cleaning properties. As the lotus unfolds each morning, it cleanses itself of dirt and debris, the filth collecting in the dew and rolling off its leaves. The texture of the lotus leaf produces a hydrophobic ability: repelling water.

I could go into further detail, expounding on the years of research I've devoted to this remarkable flower. I could also illustrate what I personally know from my own experience: the silky feel of the petals when submerged, the way the stalks cling to hair. How, despite the beauty on the water surface above, just below is a dark, desolate world—a shadow world—void of life. Where the stalks twine and trap like a spider's legs, and no matter how hard you fight to escape, you're forever entombed.

A shiver crawls along my skin, and I hit Enter to start a new line.

It's a warped piece of irony, for such beauty on the surface is terrifying beneath.

You can love and fear a thing all at once.

I stop rocking and swipe the mouse pad, toggling the computer screen from one document page to the other. I do it again. Back and forth.

Two documents are open on my Mac. Two incomplete novels. One has been incomplete for years. The other is a shiny new, blank page.

My fingers probe for the rubber band around my wrist. I roll the pads of my fingers over the band as I think, then I flip back to the previous document and continue.

I read a proverb—though I can't recall by whom—that states knowledge dispels fear. Trepidation only exists because we do not understand what we fear. That, by uncovering the mystery, we slay our demons.

This is my only hope as I endeavor to be as pure as the beautiful lotus that haunts me.

That's about as poetic as I'll get on the subject. I've made many attempts to describe the lotus, what it signifies to me, since nothing scientific does it justice. I fail every time. And truthfully, my inability to describe what the lotus means to me goes much deeper than mere word choice.

There's a boiler of shame holding me back.

Truth is, I'm not a botanist. I'm not a scientist. And after failing to complete my major, sadly, I'm not a psychologist, either.

I'm a true crime writer.

And as a writer, I'm allowed to take certain creative liberties. Transforming people's very real lives, their experiences, their pain and sorrow—that which I sharpen myself against—into a story. Readers want the truth. But they also want the fiction.

That's what sells books.

My publisher sells a lot of books.

The word *deadline* has become one I loathe.

I tell myself the deadlines are what keep me from completing my own story, uncovering my own mystery... but after all this time, it's getting harder to swallow that lie.

Deep breath, and I flip over to the newest document.

The Delany murder. *What is the mystery?* I ask the blank page.

I push back in my glider, stare at the screen. The white page with the little blinking curser, a taunt. Writer's block, I don't believe in it. It's a lame excuse we writers rely on when the simple truth is we've lost the imagination.

No, I'm not blocked—I'm sidetracked.

This is not my story.

In order to weave a tale around the Delany murder, one needs all the pieces. I don't have them. Not yet. For now, there's a human element missing. Some facet of the victim or even the killer that is required to reveal the humanity.

Fine. Invent it—that's what I do.

In Her Wake is the first book to investigate the

gruesome Delany murder, and the woman behind the mystery...

I write for half an hour, filling three pages with psych terms and raw, gritty details of the crime scene. Because, although that's all I have at this point, I need to start the story somewhere. Even before I have the facts, before I fully immerse myself in the investigation, I need a glimpse into my opinion—as this is also how readers will first perceive the victim.

I do this because my editor says I have a difficult time relating to people. She's being polite, when what she actually means is people have a hard time relating to *me*. She claims my writing, although good, is stilted in the emotions department. Therefore, my first drafts are more technical, and my writing leaves her feeling distanced, removed from the characters.

At least, that's the feedback I got from my editor before she shredded my first book. I suppose it was the right choice, because that novel went on to hit the best-seller's list.

Sometimes, when I'm reading her notes, I feel like a fraud.

Her: *"More insight into the victim's past."*

Her: *"More depth—give us raw emotion here."*

And so on and so on.

Then there's the question of whether or not a writer of truth should weave themselves into the narrative. I wondered this from the start, when I first began my descent into the realm of true crime writing. Every writer—whether of fact or fiction—imbues the pages with a part of themselves. It's impossible not to. We slip into our characters, the dialogue, the prose. Like a thief, we creep onto the scene, hoping no one will notice.

Only how much of oneself belongs in someone else's story? I find it's like walking a tightrope. Too much of the author's narrative, and we're regarded as indulgent. Too little, and we're labeled pretentious, boring, or worse, derivative.

My argumentative reply to my editor: *the author cannot be the story.*

Yet, in order to create a brutally honest work, there must be layers of the author, bared, unvarnished. Exposed. Vulnerable. Woven throughout the story seams.

I envy those who demonstrate this talent so effortlessly.

Stretching my neck, I work out the kink, then brace my fingers over the keys. "Dig deep." My editor's advice still fresh, I write the best intro I can with my limited emotional range.

This is the victim's truth.

As blood bloomed the murky water, pain sliced her insides, cold crushed her chest. Icy water filled her lungs.

My fingers halt over the keyboard. I stop rocking.

Was the water cold for the victim?

A flitting wisp of a memory assaults me, then it's gone. A cruel tease. Trying to hold on to a sudden flash from the past is like trying to grip a wiggling fish. My mind knows the memory will cause pain, so it quickly rids itself of the thought. Throwing the fish back in the lake.

Lake.

There it is again, the floating lotus bobbing up into my mind.

You don't belong here.

Dammit. This is the third time I've attempted to begin this book, only to be sucked down by the undertow of the past. It's why *the book* is open on my Mac now. Why I can't quit toggling between documents.

The victim's death is too similar.

I should've said no to this project.

I snap the rubber band against my inner wrist as I focus on the differences between the crimes. There were no lotuses at the victim's crime scene. I checked. It's the first thing I look for when a floater case comes across my proverbial desk.

The Delany case is the first drowned victim cold case I've agreed to work.

"We don't have to take this case…"

Special Agent Rhys Nolan said this to me two weeks ago, and my answer at the time was: "If we don't, who will?"

Now, I'm wondering if his concern was valid, whether he was right to question if it would hit too close to home. The victim was discovered floating near the shore of a lake, stabbed. Drowned. Only a hundred miles separation between my crime scene and hers.

I would have to be inhuman not to feel a connection— not to *see* a connection.

But I'm getting ahead of myself. Looking for patterns that aren't there.

According to the medical examiner's report, the victim was stabbed eight times. Rib cage to pelvis. Although that is an alarming near resemblance, Rhys would point out the disparities. The biggest of which is: There was no lateral laceration to her sternum.

As for the absent white lotuses… The crime scene

landscape is not an indicator; it's based on the MO, or motive. The kill method. The victimology.

Which I've pursued all before in search of my killer. I've exhausted the parameters.

Against my acutely logical disposition, I even sought out a dream interpreter. To see if they could knock loose the suppressed memories. It failed, of course. My dream was not a premonition. It was conjured out of fear—fear of losing Drew.

I don't believe in omens.

Past and present touch at different moments in our lives, like a blade of grass arcing in on itself. Events repeating. A scene already lived in a dream. Some refer to this as deja vu. Or a past life experience.

I find if I explore hard enough, I can always find an explanation.

Like Baader-Meinhof phenomenon; frequency illusion. My mind tries to form a pattern because it's engineered to do so. After the attack, I saw white lotuses everywhere. They haunted me.

Of course, I lived in Florida. Phenomenon or inevitability?

Clearly, I'm not sentimental. I don't give credence to fate or chance, and most phenomena can be explained away. Like, I probably never noticed them as much before. Prior to the event, a white lotus held no significance for me. It's as simple as that.

So I've accepted my new quest. Knowledge. Enlightenment. To uncover the mystery. If not for me, for others—to solve the riddle and bring them closure.

This is how I got into true crime writing. Documenting closure is as close to the real thing as I may ever get.

I shake out my hands, blow a forceful breath from my lungs. "It's not my story." I'll keep uttering these words, like a rehearsal. "It's about finding the victim's killer." *Not mine*.

Because that's the missing part, the link. The jagged puzzle piece that will eventually slip into place, giving me that moment of completion. Peace.

I start a new paragraph.

How did he select her?

The killer's link to the victim is always a mystery... until it's not. Like the ending to almost any story, it's never very imaginative. Wrong place, wrong girl. What other reason could anyone have in taking Joanna Delany from this world in such a cruel way?

Rhys and I will link the killer to the victim. No matter how tenuous, there's always a nexus. They may have never crossed paths before, or they may have seen each other every day. No matter where the maze starts, both killer and victim are connected on a visceral level now. They are connected in a way that most people will never fully understand.

This thought consumes me, and I stare at the page on the screen, not really seeing it. The screen wavers at the edges, and I blink hard. Rub my eyes.

A flash of his hand reaching through the water...and then it's gone.

This time, I set my laptop on the hardwood floor and trek to my cluttered desk, grabbing a sheet from the printer tray.

I sketch an outline of the flower, its stalk descending into the depths like a wiry tentacle. I recall, in that fleeting moment, thinking how rare it was to see a red lotus. It wasn't red, of course. White tinged with my blood, a death filter, the inky color clouding the water.

My hand stills over the outline of a man, his features blank. A throb pulses at my temples as I strain to recall...

Nothing.

Sometimes, when this moment surfaces in a dream, the face is of Officer Dutton. The first person I recall seeing afterward, when I awoke in the hospital room. Other times it's Drew, my college professor and ex-boyfriend. The face takes on different features, different people from my life, always elusive.

I curse and set the pencil down.

Today is no different.

"Just another day," I say aloud, to the only other being in my small house.

Lilly wraps her slender cat body along the glider footstool, her long tail coiling around the leg. She's all black with a little pink nose. During the first year *after*, I found the silence the most unbearable part. As a kitten, Lilly chased away the quiet, brought life to my very dead existence.

Following my physical recovery, I did seek mental help. Another way to free the trapped memory of that night, but it proved useless. All the psychologist wanted to talk about was my feelings and coping mechanisms. Utterly useless to my case.

Yet, Dr. Lauren did say one thing that resonated with me: *We're all connected.*

Because of this, I often envision the submerged, wiry stalks and vines all entwined at the bottom of the lake as everyone from my past. All linked in that dark, underwater world. Secrets trapped.

Where I left them.

I glance up, sneaking a glimpse of the murder board. A neurotic action from when I was obsessed with solving my case. A while ago, I draped a sheet over the whiteboard to hide the names and curb the compulsion.

I've related to people differently my whole life. This, along with my failed memory, was an obstacle. An exploration into the human condition started me on a quest to uncover people and their connections to me before the event. That's why I started *the book*.

At first, I worked diligently on my case to find the truth.

I thought a lot about Drew. How his actions led to that night. Was my young, naïve love for my psych professor the catalyst, or was he more centric?

Or maybe Chelsea was the first tipped domino. Showing up at his door to announce her pregnancy catapulted me right into the arms of a killer.

After nearly four years, I'm not any closer to narrowing it down than the case detectives were then.

I have come to only one conclusion. Life is a twisted web of people and their actions.

And we're all at fault.

My laptop sounds with the Skype jingle. I twirl my hair into a bun at my nape as I head to the glider, then plant my Mac on my lap. Rhys's image fills the app screen.

I accept the call. "Hale, what's the progress on the Delany case?"

No greeting. No formalities. I appreciate this about the agent.

"Uh, witness accounts are sketchy at best." I set the

laptop on the footstool and grab a binder from the floor, leafing through the pages. "They were sketchy a year ago, to be honest. Of course, I did question the dog walker and the neighbor couple from the complex over the phone as an 'investigative journalist', so they may need a more authoritative voice in law enforcement to interview them for new leads."

"All right. Agreed," Rhys says. "Have you contacted the mother yet?"

I glance up from the reports. No use making excuses; I'm an open book to Rhys. "No. I'd rather you do so."

He brings the phone screen closer so I can see him clearly. "I want you to get comfortable talking to family members," he says. "You have to get over your aversion."

"It's not an aversion, per se." Out of his view, I snap the band at my wrist. "I know my limitations. Family interviews are too important."

"Yeah, you're right. That awkward throat clearing thing you do really grates on people's nerves."

I twist my mouth sardonically. "Thanks."

His mouth tips into a smile. "You're the one who values honesty. I'm happy to feed you flattering lies, instead."

I shake my head, moving on. "Could they have overlooked anyone?" By this, I'm referring to the assigned homicide detectives on the Delany case a year ago.

He quirks an eyebrow. He's attractive in that brutally cliché FBI agent way. If he didn't care so much about solving cases and righting wrongs, he could star in his very own criminal justice TV show.

"It's always possible," he confirms. "I'd have to canvass the neighborhood and place of employment myself, go door-to-door." He releases a lengthy breath. "Lot of man hours."

Too quick for him to notice, hopefully, I glance around my empty house—empty all except for Lilly. "I can be there by tonight. My man hours are cheap."

He pulls his most contemptuous look. The Federal Bureau of Investigation comps the travel fair, but it's Rhys who has to suffer the ungodly stack of paperwork. "I can't do much more from Missouri," I add. "We really need to question everyone again, and find out if the locals missed anything the first time around." Which, not to rag on small-town cops, but they usually do. It's politics. Not enough men, not enough pay, to work a murder case like this.

Rhys concedes. "Might take a week, tops." A flash of commiseration, then he says what's really bothering him about this field trip. "It's Florida, Hale. Are you all right with that?"

The bobbing lotuses rise up, and I tamp them down. Back into the murky depth where they have resided.

"I'll be fine. Besides, Florida is a big state. West Melbourne is like, a hundred miles away from all that."

All that.

My murder. My death.

Killer never caught.

Rhys nods uneasily. "All right, then. See you tonight. Be safe."

I pack quickly. I book a flight, order an Uber, and call my elderly neighbor to inquire if she can cat sit. She can, and so I give Lilly a thorough brush down before I leave, the sun just dipping behind the tree-lined horizon.

At the airport, I fiddle with my keys as I await the boarding of my flight. Twirling the gray fob around the key ring, I stare at the USB drive I keep clipped to my key chain. The unfinished manuscript—*the book*—resides within the digital code. It goes with me everywhere. After my case officially went cold, I thought that, if I couldn't solve my murder, then I could at least tell my story. I would purge it from my system. Cleanse my leaves like the lotus.

But as I delved into that night, I realized I had very few facts. Worse, my memories never fully recovered. They're a patched quilt of the sad and macabre moments that led up to the event.

The event.

My editor is right. I even distance myself *from* myself, referring to the brutal attack that took my life for sixty-seven seconds in an obscure way.

Regardless, I couldn't complete my story because I had no idea why I was targeted, and no clues as to whom the perpetrator was. So instead, I dove into true crime novels and read others' stories. Getting small, gratifying glimpses of other victims and their closed cases.

Closure. I was starved for it.

That spurred me to start my own investigation into other unsolved cases, and the numbers were staggering. Statistically, one-third of murder cases go unsolved. Television and movies would have the public believe otherwise.

And maybe that's not such a bad thing, making would-be murderers think twice before committing the act if he or she believes they won't get away with it.

That was not the case for my attacker, however.

That person found me at my most vulnerable and struck.

A familiar ache blooms beneath my breastplate. Muscle memory, sparked by thought, of slashed ligaments and bone. The wounds healed, but my mind won't let me forget. The phantom pain triggered by anxiety, stress. Anger.

Likely the most significant reason as to why I'm unable to solve my own case. I'm too psychologically connected. In the time that Rhys and I have worked together, I've helped solve six cold cases. One becoming a best-selling novel. With a second book slated to release in six months. But the emotional blinders go on when I stare into my past.

The closer I get to Florida, the more alive the pain becomes. A greeting from my former life.

Welcome home.

❧ 3 ❧

BOOK OF CHELSEA

LAKIN: THEN

He wanted her the way I wanted to be her.

Envy is a powerful and debilitating emotion. Stunting, all consuming. Jealousy can twist you into a gnarled creature, bent on self-destruction. Though at the time I felt powerless, as if the tighter I held on, the quicker the wispy tendrils slipped through my fingers.

I was losing Drew.

I saw it in his eyes. When he looked at her, called her name. He coveted her.

I coveted her life. Sitting three rows behind Chelsea, I positioned myself so I could see the way she tossed her blond hair, the way she chewed on her pen cap, the way her temples creased when she laughed at his jokes.

She was every man's fantasy. And every woman's nightmare.

But it was so much more than that; I craved to know more...look beneath the topical veneer she displayed for others, and dissect her. Open her up so I could learn what made her tick. How she appeared to be so open, made everyone around her love and hate her at the same time, while fearing being rejected by her.

She was a study into everything that I wasn't.

I was attending the University of Central Florida on scholarship. Her affluent parents made donations to the school. I was poised at one end of the spectrum, and she the other—a much better fit for Drew. His own family held in high regard, knowing his doctorate would—*finally*—launch him to the proper level, where he would no longer *have* to teach.

I majored in psychology. A senior, Chelsea was auditing the class. If I didn't stop comparing myself to her, Drew said, I was going to drive myself crazy. There was nothing between them. It was all in my head. She wasn't his type. He flattered her because their families moved in the same circles. He had to be polite. Besides, she was a student.

So am I, I wanted to say.

Insecurity is not attractive to men.

But I couldn't help myself. Couldn't stop the obsessive thoughts. If I thought about it enough, somehow, I would prevent it from happening. Like wishing on a star; those dreams never came true.

I knew she wanted him, in the way beautiful girls want men, so they can toss them aside afterward. Their stamp on the man's backside like a grade of meat: *processed*.

Me, on the other hand, I believed I had something special with Drew. I wasn't outgoing. I was reserved, difficult to connect with, and Drew broke through my defenses. He swept in and shone a light on my dark little corner, and the fear of losing that intimacy…

I couldn't lose him, or what we had. The dread of it hollowed me out inside, and I felt sick, helpless.

As much as I loathed what Chelsea was doing, I also hated myself for what her presence in my life was doing to me, flaunting my past, that other girl *before* Drew, right in my face. In a way, she reminded me of Amber—how my cousin's vibrant, charismatic personality stole the spotlight.

I was always second to Amber. As kids, she demanded all attention on her. But I loved her, my best friend, and I was content to at least follow in her shadow. I was shy back then, but it wasn't until she was gone that I became withdrawn.

Without Amber's light, I didn't want to see the world.

That's why, this time, I can't let Chelsea win.

Amber would make me stand up for myself.

I push the unhealthy feelings down, down. *Breathe.* Drew has helped me overcome so much; he's opened me up in a way that I never experienced before, and when I'm finally on the cusp of sloughing off the rest of the dead shell encasing me, Chelsea swirls onto the stage, a self-indulgent twister wreaking havoc.

Class dismissed, I lingered near the doorway, pretending to check messages. I watched her lean over his desk, twirl her hair, her trilling laugh drowning out the rapid beat of my heart. I closed my eyes.

One more week.

Just another week and Drew and I would be leaving for spring break. Together. Away from temptations and fears.

I'd have his undivided attention. I'd rekindle the spark that seemed to dwindle over the past couple of months.

The longer I watched them together, the more helpless I felt. They looked good. A perfect fit. Desperation slithered in through my widening cracks.

I have to stop this from happening.

But my dream, still fresh, mocked me. I'd already seen how this ends.

As Chelsea passed me, she tossed her hair, the ends smacking my cheek.

I still remember the strawberry scent of her hair.

❧ 4 ❧

COLD CASE

LAKIN: NOW

Here's what we know about the Delany case:

On Friday, March 23rd, 2018, at approximately 9:45pm, Joanna Delany was discovered dead at Lucent Lakes West. Joseph Meyer (pseudonym) was walking his dog (chocolate lab) on the pathway that abuts a man-made lake when he spotted what he first thought to be an animal washed up in the reed grass.

The curious lab directed their course toward the body, and Joseph muttered a profanity when he realized it was a naked woman floating near the bank (according to his statement). There was no question if she was dead: her pale body was encased in mud and grass. Her skin bloated, opaque eyes wide and vacant. Joseph forced his dog away from the scene and dialed 9-1-1 from the pathway.

Officer Leon Brady, a patrol officer with the WMPD (West Melbourne Police Department), responded to the call. Upon Officer Brady's arrival, he radioed the precinct to request the on-duty homicide detective. Then he proceeded to question Joseph and take his statement.

Detective Orson Vale and trainee detective Allen Right ordered CSU to rope off the area around the victim and backside of the lake within ten minutes of their arrival to the crime scene. Detective Vale then requested the medical examiner and proceeded to inspect the scene and question the witness himself.

What followed, according to the reports, was standard procedure in a homicide investigation. No glaring mistakes of protocol or oversights stand out. But no foremost insight from either detective or major crimes, either.

The first hours in a murder investigation are crucial. Most of your pertinent information comes in during the first twenty-four hours on the case. Victim ID. Next of kin. Cause of death. The trifecta to help point the way to the prime suspect.

Which, during the first two days of the investigation, according to Detective Vale's report, was the boyfriend. It's always the love interest, until he can be cleared.

Jamison Smith cooperated with the locals and was cleared within forty-eight hours with an alibi. Though not an ideal alibi, personal judgment shouldn't overshadow an investigation. Jamison's lover, Kimberly Towell, had definitive proof of Jamison's whereabouts for the estimated time of death of his girlfriend. He was with Kimberly. Handcuffed to her bedpost. There's a video to prove it.

Long exhale. Flip the page.

Cases that involve cheating trigger a negative response in me. Of course, I try not to let my personal feelings muddy the water, but I'm human. I'm going to have human emotions and reactions to details that pluck a sensitive nerve.

And sometimes, those things that make us human can even further the investigation.

It's all how you look at it.

Right now, sitting in Orlando Melbourne International, brushing up on the facts of the case, I'm looking at the case too personally already.

I hate this godforsaken state.

As I'm putting away my binder, I spot Agent Nolan through the glass-sliding doors. Seeing him is like coming home in a way that Florida will never hold for me again. I stand to meet him, and with a slight nod, he grabs my carry-on and we're off. No time for pleasantries; there's a case to solve.

It's truly what I like best about him.

How I met Special Agent Rhys Nolan:

My case went cold around the six-month mark. Honestly, it was cold well before then, but that was when Detective Dutton officially threw his hands in the air. When leads halt, and officials are at a loss for where to take the investigation, the case goes cold. That doesn't mean that my case was closed—unsolved cases are never officially closed—they remain open. Just set aside.

Every detective I've interviewed has admitted to working on cold cases in their free time. What little free time they have, that is. For them, they've said, it's a compulsion, a driving need to break out the files and go over the cases at least once a year, to see if the distance allows them to view things in a new light. Discover some piece of the puzzle they missed.

No one was driven to compulsively work on my case.

After six months, the understaffed and overworked Leesburg PD declared the Cynthia Marks (my given name) case cold. I was set aside for more pressing investigations, like the local drug ring.

I was alive, after all. Detective Dutton wasn't trying to solve a murder. There were no similarities between my attack and any others around the Lake County area; there was no pressing concern to prevent a future attack.

The return calls from the department heads and detectives became fewer and fewer. The lengthy pauses on the line dragging out longer. Soon I didn't bother with the routine calls seeking updates.

My case was dead.

My parents were content to let it go. Talking about the event only caused them anxiety, pain. I wasn't Amber. I hadn't become lost to them like she had. Their daughter, their only child, had survived. They weren't pursuing justice. I no longer involved them in my obsessive search.

I turned my focus to other cases with similar MOs. I expanded the search radius. Maybe my attacker wasn't a local. Maybe it wasn't a personal assault. It's possible the assailant moved from city to city in Florida, attacking young women. And no one looked close enough to connect the dots.

For Agent Nolan, working in the FBI's cold case division didn't happen willingly. At the age of twenty-nine, Rhys was injured in the field. Gunshot to the thigh. His injury benched him for nearly a year, where he worked hard at recovery in order to be reinstated as a field agent.

We had this in common.

My recovery took me on a different course, also. All the way to Missouri. With a new name, new identity, and a new career path. A self-imposed—*inflicted*—witness protection program.

Agent Nolan would never be a field agent again. And I would never complete my degree to become a psychologist. By some divine twist of irony, due to our failures, our paths crossed.

I placed a call to the FBI cold case division and spoke with a sullen Agent Nolan who had no time for paranoid victims. Later that week, a knock at my door, and there stood the sullen agent, case file in hand.

I was his first official cold case.

Rhys claims that what changed his mind was one thing: victims rarely get the chance to tell their story. So many times he wished he could ask the dead their secrets. Now, this was his chance.

Maybe I should've been offended about the comparison. But I was, in fact, neither dead nor living when we met. I was found on the lake's muddy bank. That dirt never washed off. By the time I left for good, I was the mud.

But, I had answers that could help solve my case, even if I didn't realize it.

After our first meeting, where he asked questions to help fill in the gaps, Rhys returned to Quantico and across the distance, we worked tirelessly on my case.

He re-interviewed witnesses from the Dock House and the Uber driver. He spoke with the local PD in my hometown, questioning the detectives assigned my case. He pored over the images of my attack. He memorized my wounds. The placement, the degree of the injuries, the depth of every laceration. Each contusion and the abrading on my skin.

Near the three-month mark of the reopened investigation, Rhys knew my scars as well as I did.

But despite our exhaustive search, we were no closer to solving the mystery as to why I was targeted one night in March. It appeared I was a victim of chance. Although the facts of the case did pull up similar MOs across the country, Rhys theorized that I might have been the perpetrator's first victim. A stranger selected because I was in the wrong place at the wrong time.

It was possible that, if I had been the first, the killer's MO had since changed.

I can't admit aloud how hopeless that possibility makes me feel.

On the one-year anniversary of my attack, Rhys convinced me to return to Silver Lake.

I had vowed never to go back…not until my attacker was apprehended…and it was a painful vow to break. We retraced my steps. From the campus to the driveway of Drew's previous home (where Chelsea told me about the pregnancy). From the apartment I shared with my roommate (where Drew and I argued and the police took my statement) to the Dock House (where my roommate tried to help me forget). Then, to the pier of the lake, not far from the Silver Lake community where my parents still live.

Rhys and I stared at the rippling reflection of the crescent moon on the water.

Lotuses blanketed the lake with a iridescent sheen.

I listened to the crickets' chirr, a haunting melody that I had no memory of from that fateful night. The wicked sound of frogs croaking filled the otherwise calm air. A desolate and eerie quietness that froze my bones.

That was the moment I revealed *him* to Rhys. The secret I'd kept from everyone—that twisted belief I had wrestled with, wanting to believe in my phantom hero some days, to deny his existence others.

The man who pulled me from the water.

The only memory—real or not—that I had from the night of my near demise.

In that moment, I wished I had Rhys's training. I wanted to look at his face and read what he was thinking. But then, I was also terrified to know.

His actions have always spoken louder than his words. His silence sliced at me like the weapon used to carve my body all those nights ago. His weighted stare bled right through me, and when he cupped my face and placed a kiss to my brow, I dissolved under that comfort.

It didn't matter if he believed me or not. Whether I had imagined it or not.

I was alive.

Man or animal, ghost or angel—whatever fished me from the lake—I had not drowned.

It was time to live.

The roll of the car engine awakens me from my post-flight trance. Inside Rhys's rented sedan, I reach for my seatbelt and buckle in, pushing the heaviness from my chest.

"Ready?" he asks.

Deep breath. I twist the band around my wrist. "I am."

𝕾 5 𝕾

BOOK OF CAMERON

LAKIN: THEN

I recall the way the room pulsed with light and color. Vibrating waves of red and blue.

I had Cameron's leather jacket draped over my shoulders. It was a humid eighty-something degrees even in the spring evening, but the biting chill of the situation was making me shiver.

"I dreamed this would happen." A mantra I kept repeating.

Chelsea's visit that day had triggered the reminder of the dream. But there was more... More twisted visions inside the dream, beckoning me closer.

A knife slashing. Red streaming. A scream wrenched from the abyss of pain.

An officer glanced my way. I couldn't focus on details —my mind unable to absorb the scene. But I remember the officer's tight frown, the way it made him appear older than he probably was. This man who had seen so little was judging my life, disapproval crawling down his features like a surly grub.

"She needs help." I heard another officer say.

Cameron was nodding, agreeing, giving her statement. My roommate just wanted the two cops out of our apartment. She hated scenes, drama. She hated eavesdropping neighbors.

It had been an eavesdropping neighbor that called the police on me and Drew.

Our fight had escalated quickly.

Heart thudding heavily in my ears, I squeezed my eyes closed. Pressure built at the back of my sockets. A threat to crack my skull.

The flashing brought on a strobe light effect of the dream. *Chelsea and a scream…dark water…* The past and present were merging into some horrid nightmare that I couldn't shake, that I couldn't wake from. I was detached, wandering through a fog.

"What the hell happened?"

Cameron knelt before me. The warmth of her hand on my knee.

She'd gotten rid of the cops. Finally, I opened my eyes, able to take a breath. I shook my head, not knowing where to start, *how* to explain to my friend.

Shouts. Breaking glass. Threats.

In the end, Cameron didn't need me to tell her what happened. Rumors were already circulating campus. Social media was abuzz with posts reveling in a tawdry affair between teacher and student.

Once she saw the first thread on her phone, she cursed.

"He's a dick." A disgusted noise escaped. "No, dicks

are at least useful. He's a douchebag." Her eyes turned soft. "Oh, Cynth. I'm so sorry."

Me too.

But not as sorry as Drew would soon be.

Should've locked him away.

When Drew became the prime suspect in my case, that's what the detective had said, though he thought I couldn't comprehend from my drug-induced state on the hospital bed.

They should've locked them both away.

🦋 6 🦋

RIVULETS

LAKIN: NOW

R hys and I, we needed a win.

After our failed trip to Silver Lake, I returned to Missouri, still fleeing a faceless, nameless killer, and I could've given up. There was nowhere to go from there. No new leads. And my brave attempt to confront my fear by visiting the scene had failed.

That moment in time was a black hole.

But I had brought something back with me.

Hope.

And depending on your mental state, hope can either be a blessed thing or a curse.

Right then, my newfound hope was a mix of both. But it was a nice departure from helplessness. While I was working my case with Rhys, I wasn't fixated on the fear. I wasn't paralyzed.

Once home, I scoured the Internet and pod casts for cold cases. I had become addicted to them. The moment I found *the one*, I sent Rhys the information. I put together a starting point, a theory, and investigative notes from the case. My journalism classes were finally coming in handy.

The agent probably won't admit it, but he needed that new case just as badly as I did. His failure to solve my case threatened him; he needed to believe, to hope, that his career as an FBI agent wasn't over. I believe that's the only reason he conceded to let me "tag along." Soon, I became a consultant for the FBI's cold case division. An unofficial team member with a very unimpressive hourly pay rate for my time.

The FBI also won't acknowledge this, but the positive publicity they got from a solved cold case turned NYT Bestseller is what keeps Agent Nolan's small team above reproach within the department.

We solved the Patterson case within two months. And it felt good. Addictive.

I wrote and completed my first novel. Sold the rights. Another written book later, the special agent and I have solved six unsolvable cases.

Neither one of us has looked at my case since.

I crack the car window, then immediately regret doing so. The humid Florida air is congested with the marshy scent of the east coast. You can throw a stone in any direction and hit a body of water. Lakes, ponds, rivers. Florida is one long peninsula slowly sinking into the ocean.

Unbidden, a wave of melancholy washes over me, and the compulsion to snap the rubber band takes hold. I scratch my wrist, antsy. A memory of Drew and I on the beach stirs, and I quickly suppress it. I hit the control to roll up the window.

As if he's reading my mind, Rhys says, "You miss it."

I change the car A/C from vent to circulate to stop the outside from seeping in. "Is that a question or an accusation?"

He doesn't laugh. Rhys rarely laughs. I spot the slight curve of his lips, though.

"Do I miss the smell?" I ask. "The muggy humidity that clings to your skin and makes you feel dirty with grime and sweat even after you've just showered?" I look out the window, at the flatness of Highway 1. "Not a chance."

I don't have to glance his way to know the grin he wears.

"I think we should hit the apartment complex first," he says, and I'm thankful for the topic change. "Canvass the neighborhood and get fresh statements."

Relieved, I agree. "First thing in the morning. Where are we staying?"

I packed quickly and jumped on a plane, knowing Rhys would handle the details of our stay. He says it's easier for him to work out the reimbursement from the bureau.

He flips the blinker and merges onto the onramp. "Holiday Inn. Between Melbourne and West Melbourne. Not too far from the crime scene, and near enough to other locations we'll need to look at."

Rhys checks us in at the front desk while I wait in the lobby, luggage and bag seated around my Converse-clad feet. When not traveling, I typically dress more professional; people have a preconceived expectation of how agents and their cohorts working an investigation should dress. If they're not distracted by your clothes—

trying to figure out if you're qualified—then they can concentrate on the facts.

Special Agent Rhys Nolan, on the other hand, always looks the part in his standard black suit and tidy, light-brown hair. I don't think I've ever seen him with facial scruff; always clean-shaven.

He likes to say: "I am the job."

I'm the job, too, but I guess writers get a little more flexibility with their wardrobe. At least I leave the pajamas at home when I'm on a case.

I bite my lip to keep from frowning. At one point in my life, on a very different course, I'd have been expected to dress the professional part. Psychologist Dr. Marks has a more professional ring to it than Lakin Hale, true crime writer. Although I suppose both avenues led me to a place where I explore the mind and behavior of criminals.

Semantics.

"All set." Rhys hands me a room card, interrupting my thoughts.

"Thanks. See you in the morning."

We go our separate ways at the end of the hallway. By the time I'm lying on the hotel bed, I've compulsively snapped my wrist twenty-six times throughout the day. Despite that, my thoughts still cling to the past.

Vista Shores apartment complex is situated across the street from the crime scene. The victim, Joanna Delany, lived in apartment 208. Her mother, Bethany Delany, lives in 213.

Rhys and I ride the elevator up to the second level.

"Jumping right into the deep end," I mutter as the *ding* of the elevator sounds. My insides flutter with the feel of the car coming to a sudden halt.

He lets me step into the hallway first. "Mothers are the hardest part," he agrees.

"You know that parents are usually the last to know what's going on in a victim's personal life."

He sighs. "Ms. Delany lived a few doors down from her daughter. Maybe they were closer than normal." He stops outside her door, cutting a glance at me. For a second, I wonder if he's insinuating something about my lack of relationship with my own parents. "Her proximity to the vic could give us more insight to her last days."

His logic makes sense. Still, I pull in a steadying breath and brace for the painful encounter. My detachment from people comes across as uncaring, heartless, or so I've been told. That doesn't work well when dealing with grieving parents.

Over the past few years, with Rhys's training on interviews, I've gotten better at concealing. Or rather, blending. I guess call it what it is: *faking*. Not the caring part—I'm not a sociopath—but conveying my sentiments.

A few seconds after Rhys knocks, Ms. Delany answers the door. Her dark complexion was probably striking once with a rich, healthy glow. Now there's a pallid, sallow hue overlaying her skin. Sunken eyes and chapped lips complete the neglected look.

"Ms. Delany. I'm Special Agent Rhys Nolan with the FBI cold case division. We spoke on the phone yesterday afternoon."

His mention of their conversation awakens the woman. "Oh, right. Of course. Come on in." She widens the door, allowing us to enter her home. "Please ignore the mess. I've been meaning to box up a lot of stuff."

She continues to make excuses for the apartment's condition as she leads us to a sofa in the living room. Rhys waves off her apologies. "You have a beautiful home."

Other than piles of folded clothes and knick-knacks lining the living room wall, the space is immaculate. Ms. Delany sits opposite us in a comforter chair, and I notice her dry, cracked hands. She cleans…all the time.

A pang twinges beneath my breastbone.

Rhys nods for me to begin. Most women find it easier to talk to another woman. At least right at first. I push Record on my phone and set it on the glass table. "Do you mind? It helps us when we can replay interviews."

Her head shakes rapidly. "That's fine. I don't mind."

With what I hope is a delicate approach, I delve into the hard questions. The things that the case detectives have already asked this mother over and over. Things she's tired of repeating, I'm sure—but we need the answers one last time, in hope of discovering new information.

"Ms. Delany…"

"Please, call me Bethany." Her smile wobbles.

I match her smile. "Bethany, who do you think did this to your daughter?"

One of the most painful questions, but also one of the most important. Rarely does a parent's bias result in an arrest, but it can lead to another person of interest. Another witness. Someone that the investigating detectives overlooked.

Her face pales. She reaches a shaky hand toward a dust rag on the table only to place it in her lap. "Jo wasn't seeing anyone at the time, other than Jamison. She wasn't like that."

She's aware that the boyfriend/husband is always the initial suspect. I wonder how many cop shows she's tortured herself watching, looking for clues on how to solve her daughter's murder.

"It doesn't have to be anyone she was intimate with," I press. "Maybe it's someone who first popped into your head but you shut it down, wondering where the thought even sprang from."

Nothing beats a mother's intuition.

Her brown eyes latch on to me and widen, as if I've revealed some secret. "Rixon," she says. "Mike Rixon…I think that was his name. He was Jo's boss at the restaurant where she worked. She'd only been there a few months, but I remember the way he looked at her one night while I was there. Just something about it didn't sit right with me." She frowns.

"Thank you, Bethany. That's very helpful." I glance at my notepad. "Can you tell us a little about Joanna's modeling career?"

I get her talking about what Ms. Delany calls "the good days." The victim's early bio was quite impressive. At the age of nineteen, Joanna was on track to become a well-known model in the industry. A rising star. Four years into her career, and the bottom fell out. It's a ruthlessly competitive, unforgiving industry, and models either make it or they don't. The older one gets, the harder it becomes to soar to the top against younger, fresher faces.

Joanna toured Europe for a brief time, shot impressive photos for women's magazines, and then suddenly, as quickly as the stardom came, the offers stopped.

It's a rags to riches to rags…to shocking death story.

My publisher will only accept true crime novels based on people who they deem will pique and hold the public's interest. Not surprisingly, a pretty face on the cover with a tragic story inking the pages is ideal. People want to be shocked and awed. But they also want to feel marginally better about their own lives by comparison to someone else's unfortunate life.

Sad, but utterly true.

I chose Joanna Delany not because she was a good fit for the publisher—but because Joanna Delany chose me. She reached out from the grave, whispered of the parallels between us, and quickly became an obsessive enigma that demanded to be solved.

Rhys jumps in with his own questions, connecting the dots, learning the victim's routine in the weeks preceding her murder.

Once the interview is complete, I stop the recording and check the log, making sure we got everything. Then we thank Bethany and make our way toward the door.

"You're that crime writer," Bethany says. I pause in the open doorway, and Rhys takes up my side. "I read your book. After Agent Nolan first reached out with the possibility of reopening the case, I looked you up. Your team has solved every cold case you two have worked on together."

Every case except one.

I look to Rhys for help. His mouth flattens into a line, eyebrows drawn. His steel-gray eyes say: *she said it's* your *team.*

Thanks.

Despite my reservations, I take hold of her weathered hands. "We're going to try our hardest," I promise her.

Her eyes sheen with unshed tears and hope.

Hope.

After a year of searching for the truth, of seeking justice for her daughter, hope has become Bethany's curse. Even when you try to sever every last thread of it, hope's gauzy web latches on to the remaining pieces of your heart. It's a painful thing to witness, when a family member cannot let go, move on.

"Thank you." She squeezes my hand before she releases me. Then the tears come. Rivulets streak her dry cheeks, like rain down a desert canyon.

The sound of the door closing echos through the narrow hallway. I walk faster toward the elevator.

I sense Rhys's towering presence behind me. "You did good back there," he says. "Closure is all we can promise. Even then, it's usually not enough. We can't bring their loved ones back from the dead."

"I know." And I do. Grieving parents have a checklist. They stay stuck on step *punish killer* for a long time, and sometimes, when it's time to move forward to the healing bullet point, they can't.

"Bethany is the purest grieving mother I've met," I say. "I hope I do her justice."

I believe to be a true crime writer, you have to respect the victim.

There's a distinct difference between the creation of a character, the process of conjuring a person out of nothing —giving them living, breathing personality—and depicting a true person on the pages.

If I kill off a fictional character, the reader may suffer, on a topical level. Until they pick up the next book.

But when making a study of people—*real* people—in order to recount their story, immersing myself in their lives, I have a responsibility to them—the victims—as well as the mourning family members and friends left behind, to share their cruel experience with the utmost respect. To be compassionate, humane.

If for no other reason than to differentiate yourself from the very real killer you're also depicting.

You need that clear line between good and evil.

I need it.

The voice of the victim, as well as the voice of those closest to the victim, are the ones who direct my narrative.

Rhys and I are silent as we descend to the ground level. When the doors open, we're in a new frame of mind.

The next bullet point on our checklist: the crime scene.

BOOK OF DREW

LAKIN: THEN

I saw him the first day of my Abnormal Psychology class. I was seated in the second row. He introduced himself as *Drew*. Not Prof. Abbot. Or even Prof. Andrew Abbot. Just Drew. He was the young teacher. The cool teacher. The one who involuntarily winked while you were talking and made you feel special.

He was giving his introductory lecture on the definition of abnormal.

"We hear that word, and instinctually, subconsciously, we place it in the negative box. Something that is abnormal is not normal, therefor it's wrong." Drew glanced around the room, making eye contact with various students. I was one of them. "I want you to free your preconceived notions. Just let them go. Abnormal doesn't denote *wrong*. Instead, think of abnormal psychology in terms of the level of interference your patient may suffer in their quality of life due to their disorder."

He was brilliant. And beautiful. A lethal combination that consumed the air around him. He drew everyone in; the gravitational pull of a black hole, but you felt light, and warmth, from his sun.

A girl in the front row raised her hand. "What about maladaptive behaviors, Drew? What's the difference between that and a mental disorder?"

I wanted to roll my eyes. This girl—the one who'd stolen his attention, with her pert, bouncy tits and pert, bouncy beach waves—should know the difference if she was registered in AP. Maybe she was in the wrong class. Stumbled in thinking it was her poetry elective.

Blondes with bouncy tits always took a poetry elective.

I mocked her, yet I envied her right from the start. The way she stood out, asked dumb questions to gain his attention. And it worked.

As she peered around the class, my heart lurched, my pulse slammed through my veins. She was stunning. Her beauty was a gut punch to every girl in the class. I felt it ripple the air; a collective domino effect.

Drew knelt in front of her desk, wrist braced on the edge. "Excellent question, uh…?"

"Chelsea."

"Mental disorders are the root. Maladaptive behaviors are unhealthy ways of coping with the disorder. Most of the time, reinforcing the illness."

As everyone here learned in Psych 101.

The uncomfortable feeling dispelled as quickly as it came. I couldn't be envious of someone as vapid as Chelsea. Still, I kept sneaking glimpses at her. Curious.

Later, when Drew chose me, when he picked me out of

a sea of vapid girls all angling to be with "the hot professor", I had no more reason to fear Chelsea.

But, as Drew would denote, obsessing over a fear is a maladaptive behavior in its own right.

Drew stood and turned his attention to the class. "A patient can have any number of coping mechanisms to deal with their symptoms." He paced the front of the room, and I loved the way he moved in his jeans. "For instance, I once treated a patient who depended on dream interpretation in order to make choices through their day. They couldn't leave the house, pay a bill, or even take a shower until I'd analyzed their dream."

Another student raised their hand. "So, you essentially had control over their choices, their life. Isn't that dangerous?"

This piqued my curiosity. I leaned in, needing to know.

"Yes. Freudian techniques can be dangerous in the wrong hands," he said. "The challenge in this particular case was to use psychoanalysis in order to get the patient to interpret their own dreams, in essence letting them guide their own life. By delving into their subconscious, we discovered the patient was, in fact, revealing repressed memories through dreams." He walked to the whiteboard and jotted a note about recovered memories.

"Think of a computer. The mind is a fascinating, intricate web. Our memories race along the spun webbing, the network, connecting to folders of cached data. But here's the difference: we don't recall our memories in perfect clarity or detail. Our minds alter those moments. Every time we look at them, they change in little ways."

He spouted psychobabble like poetry. He made you

feel like he was talking directly to you, intimate. Personable.

I knew I'd fall in love with him that first day.

And I knew—somewhere in the racing neurons of my brain—that love would destroy me.

❧ 8 ❧

OPEN ENDING

LAKIN: NOW

As with an author of fiction, every true crime writer has their own style, their own voice, along with their own story to tell. We strive in our research on the case, the killer, the victims. We endeavor to reveal, essentially, our path to the truth.

Whether or not the case is solved, whether or not the killer is caught, varies. Every book is different just as every person is different. Like a fingerprint, each book is unique.

Some writers lay the facts out and lead readers on a quest for that truth with one major theory, expounding on the details until they've made their case, like a lawyer arguing before a jury. In the end, the writer hopes to prove their theory and convince readers.

For me, it wasn't enough to investigate and hammer down a theory. I wanted—*needed*—a resolution. I craved to look into the eyes of the killer once caught. To know he had stolen life for the very last time. He had met his finality.

Of course, this must happen from a safely removed distance. Poring over Internet images of perpetrators in handcuffs from my dark living room. Watching clips as officers walk them through the doors of a jailhouse. This is also why writing under a pseudonym is important. The "bad guys" can't have access to the author. It's dangerous, but it's also…

Succinct satisfaction.

Then it starts all over again.

I'll pull out my box of files and start the dig. Seeking the next case.

It's a drug. Once I experienced that first moment of completeness after we closed the Patterson case, it didn't take long before the hunger returned, more ravenous than before. I have an insatiable desire that I fear will never be sated, no matter how many murderers we catch.

I'm not oblivious. My major in psychology gave me a pretty healthy insight into myself; not allowing me the excuse of denial. My own unsolved case is sitting on the backburner, boiling over, demanding attention.

It won't let me experience relief for very long.

Not every case becomes a book. But every case *must* be solved. That's the unspoken promise Rhys and I made to each other after we shut my file permanently.

The USB drive on my key chain feels weighty in my pocket. The incomplete book a heavy burden to constantly lug around.

I'm an open ending.

I hate open endings.

The only thing in my control is the next case. The next

victim. Like Joanna Delany. She deserves my complete focus, not my pity, or *self*-pity. I'm here and she's not.

Lucent Lake West is muggy. Mosquitos already abuzz before noon. I spray my arms with repellant and hand the bottle to Rhys. Just another thing I don't miss about living in Florida.

"I remember when the mosquito truck used to drive down our street," I say, staring out over the flat lake top. The wind picks up briefly and feathers a current of ripples across the surface. "My mother would scream at me to run inside, or else I'd die from breathing the fumes." I smile at the memory, though it's rather morbid.

Amber and I had been playing in my backyard one day, climbing the orange tree, when we spotted the mosquito truck. We raced each other down the tree. She let me win. I know this, because she was faster, more agile.

I fell and broke my wrist trying to beat her, anyway.

That was the moment I absolutely acknowledged I could not win against the Ambers of the world.

As Rhys puts the bottle of spray in my bag, I slip my sleeve up and snap the band around that wrist.

"I didn't realize there was such a thing as mosquito trucks," he says as he pulls up the crime scene photos on his tablet.

I raise an eyebrow. "Lucky you."

A tight-lipped smirk rims his mouth. Rhys once told me he grew up on the northwest peninsula. It rains in that part of the country more than any other, and the winters are cold and harsh. Must be what gives him such a warm personality. I deliver my own knowing grin in return.

He hands me the tablet. "Medical examiner placed the time of death around eight p.m. This isn't the most secluded spot." He glances around the marsh scenery. "Yet she went unnoticed for over twenty-four hours before the dog walker called it in the next evening."

Sometimes it's difficult to follow his train of thought, but I latch on to his theory in this instance. "Someone familiar with the victim's schedule or the area, to know she'd be alone, and that they'd have enough time. Her mother said she used to walk in the evenings almost every day. She used it to decompress after work." Part of the victim's extended sobriety program as a recovered meth addict.

Ms. Delany was hesitant to go into details, regardless that she knows it's already in her daughter's file. Drug addiction is a storm that tears through a family. Time doesn't heal all wounds.

Rhys nods and looks at the apartment complex that abuts the lake. "The police only canvassed neighbors in the complex where the vic lived. What about the others? There are three apartment buildings that surround the lake area."

"Maybe a witness that didn't come forward," I reason aloud. "And anyone within close proximity could learn her routine."

"Let's walk the perimeter. See if we can tell which apartments are in view of the crime scene." Rhys starts toward the bank.

Before I follow his lead, I look at the tablet in my hand, at the image displayed on the screen. My chest prickles as a sinister awareness slithers over me.

Last night, I was able to get through most of the case file while lying in the hotel bed. The reports describe the body in grisly candor, but actually seeing the mutilation is different; it stirs a visceral reaction.

With a guarded breath, I zoom in on the laceration that stretches the length of her rib cage. Despite the bloated skin, the washed out, paled appearance, I can imagine what it would look like—*feel* like—once healed, had the victim lived through the attack.

It's not the same placement, or size…but the sight of the injury spikes my blood like a shot of alcohol. Dizzy, I lower the tablet.

"Dammit." Air fights its way into my lungs, and I swallow past the constriction of my throat. I stumble over a mound of reed grass, my legs shaky. "Rhys…" He doesn't hear me. "Agent Nolan!"

This stops him on the shore. He looks back at me, his suit jacket flapping open as a breeze crosses the lake. His features pull together in question.

I hold up the tablet when I reach him. "Did you see this?"

His hands go to his hips, pushing his jacket open farther. "Hale, what are you talking about?"

"This—" I point to the victim on the screen. "The ME report didn't record this laceration correctly. Did you know about it? Did you see this image?" The accusation in my tone startles even me. I draw in a breath. "Am I crazy?"

His frown deepens as he squints against the noon sun. Then his eyes find mine. "You're not crazy."

My relief is momentary.

"But," he continues, "I asked if you were comfortable taking this case." It comes across accusatory.

I drop the tablet by my thigh. "That's not—"

"I read the report. Studied the images. I asked you before," he stresses.

"Stop. This isn't about my reaction. Don't analyze me.

There's a distinct similarity here." Now that the words are out there, I can't take them back.

At his intense silence, I look past him, out to the ripples sheeting the lake.

Take it back.

But I can't. The remembered pain surges to life, bigger than this moment.

Rhys draws closer. Mercifully, he doesn't make me elaborate. He doesn't need me to. He's seen this reaction before. In victims.

"Hale, look at me."

I force my gaze away from the lake, but it's difficult to look into his knowing eyes. Still, I make myself do it, to face the cold truth.

His jawline is tense. A muscle feathers along his cheek. He's holding back. "Are you seeing a similarity?" he finally asks.

I shake my head. "I don't know."

My mind flips through my psych classes. One of the signs of late onset schizophrenia is seeing patterns where they don't exist. Then there's frequency illusion. Baader-Meinhoff phenomenon. It's also a sign of stress. Like when a person is working a cold case that resembles their attack.

Simplest, most logical explanation. Stress.

"Focus on me. Right here," he says, directing my gaze to his eyes. Something flashes in his steely gaze, and he takes hold of the tablet. He zooms in on the laceration. "What does the ME report read?"

"Length of laceration is six inches, though it could be longer. And the case file didn't have a photo from this angle. Maybe the pathologist measured wrong…"

"There are going to be similarities between this case and yours," he says. "Certain familiarities that are going to make you uncomfortable, to react. No one will judge you if you can't handle this case." He swallows, and I watch the dip along his throat. "I won't judge you."

Pressure builds at my temples. I scratch my wrist. "I can handle it."

He releases a heavy breath. "We should've gone over the case together before we hit the crime scene."

"I'm fine, Rhys." I catch my lip between my teeth, and his gaze lowers, sending a jolt of awareness through me. We're too close.

As always, he's able to sense my unease. He steps back, giving me space. He nods once, like he's answering some unspoken question within himself. Then: "First thing I did was cover every similarity and search out every disparity. I made sure. Similar, but not our guy. If I thought, even for a second, that it could be related—"

"I know," I say, forcing his words to stop. I drag my fingers through my hair as I look up at him. "Similar. But not a match to the MO." Joanna's clothes were removed. A very distinct difference for the perpetrator. "This isn't about me or my case."

"Do you believe that?"

"The victim suffered eight stab wounds to the torso focused on the abdomen, all in varying degrees of depth." As I say this, his gaze flicks to my chest, and I feel as if he can see right through the sheer material, see the scars. I cross my arms. "The fatal wound was a stab delivered to the left side of the chest that severed her pulmonary artery and lung. Cause of death, drowning."

I break it down, reciting the report like a pathologist;

clinical, detached. This puts the case into perspective, separating facts from sentiment.

I suffered ten stab wounds. One profound laceration to my sternum. I died from trauma resulting in pulmonary edema. The most likely reason for my inability to recall the attack.

Rhys studies me closely. "This isn't like you."

I swipe at the loose wisps of hair battering my face. "I know."

It's been proven; I'm not an emotional person by nature. Even after my attack, I couldn't be brought to tears. I wasn't choked up by violence on TV. The news didn't make me lose my faith in humanity. Rhys knows this about me, and he knows this outburst of…whatever it is, is out of character.

I haven't cried since Amber.

I drag in a breath. "The crime scene image jarred me. That's all." It's all I can admit.

He appears unsure at first, but then he accepts my excuse. "We can still go back."

"No. I want to work this case. Joanna deserves to have us both on it."

From my periphery, I watch Rhys lift and drop his hand. Maybe a moment where he thought about touching me, comforting me. He curls it into a fist by his side. "All right." He glances around. "Looks like the third floor of the middle building, and the third and fourth of the last building could have a good viewpoint. We have some ground to cover."

And like that, the discussion is dropped. Unless I push the topic, Rhys will end it right here.

As we navigate the shore, I snap pictures of the

buildings. I tag any apartments in view of the crime scene with notes to further look into. Later, when I'm writing this scene, I'll omit the conversation with Rhys. No one knows Cynthia or what happened to her. Lakin writes from a place of passion to uncover the truth. That's her story.

We round the bend, the reeds overgrown and the marshy smell overpowering, and that's when I see them.

Lotuses.

White and floating atop the gray lake. The flowers bob in the wake like a rolling satin sheet.

Oh, God.

Rhys is already rushing to me. I'm not expressive, but Rhys is even less so—he doesn't touch; he respects boundaries. But his hands are on me, making a physical, grounding connection.

"Let's go," he says, his voice guttural, urgent. "Don't look."

I can't stop staring at the white petals. "They weren't here before."

He doesn't respond, but he doesn't need to. The crime scene images taken at the time had no flowers. The reports made no mention. The lotuses are new—someone planted them here. Someone placed those awful flowers right over the place where the victim drowned.

❧ 9 ❧

BOOK OF CAMERON

LAKIN: THEN

Real memory or recovered memory? You might think: what's the difference? A memory is a memory. Here's the difference with recovered memories. They're not always accurate. It's like code. There's a sequence to events, and when the mind can't recall certain details, it looks at the events before and after to splice together the most logical sequence to fill the holes.

So what actually happened will be different than how my mind attempts to fill in the gaps.

I've been padding the blanks with what others tell me occurred, and what the case detectives—with years of experience—have deduced.

Below is my recount of that night to the best of my ability:

The thump of reggae music imbued the night air of the Dock House. White string lights dotted the blackness above like a starlit canopy. It was beautiful, and in my distraught state, I swayed to the slow rhythm on a barstool, trying my damndest to forget.

Everything.

Cam had convinced me to go to my parents' house. To get away from campus. On our way to Silver Lake, she took a detour; a quick stop at a bar to drink away my sorrows.

I chased the burn of heartache with soda. Then I chased the carbonated sweetness with water. Though Cam thought the shot glass held Vodka. I was there for her as much as she was there for me. This was her attempt to cheer me up. I was trying, but I'd never been a drinker. Hell, I'd never been drunk before. But admitting to that would have made me feel even more awkward, and I just longed for a moment of normalcy.

I shivered as the night's warmth blanketed my body. It was a generic kind of comfort.

Cameron stood at the end of the bar top, flirting her way to another round of shots from the bartender. His name… Tony? Tyler? I waved it off, as if blowing off any of the random guys that had hit on us that night. Except by that point, there weren't too many around.

The night was winding down. It was the official spring break kickoff, and all the campuses had executed a mass exodus to more southern locations, where they could drink and party and revel in debauchery far from here.

The few sad stragglers left behind were trying to keep the party going. A couple making out near the bar gazebo. Two military guys at a table downing beer, obviously looking for loose spring break chicks in the wrong place. A lone, partied-out drunk man leaned up against a beam.

We were a pathetic bunch. Desperate not to let the

night end, because we didn't want to face the next day. At least, in my current state, that's how I viewed the world around me.

Cam set a shot glass with amber liquid before me. "Last one. Torrance is closing shop."

Torrance. I snapped my fingers. Although emotionally and physically numb, my finger and thumb didn't quite connect. "I couldn't remember his name." I pretended to throw back the tequila, sending it over my shoulder, then glanced at Cam. "You should go home with him."

I was done with pretending for the night.

She scoffed. "Yeah, that's just what I need."

"I'm serious. He's hot. And you sacrificed your spring break in Cancun for me." I frowned. "Go. Have some fun. Make bad choices."

Her gaze captured the bartender, and I could tell she wanted him. Her devotion to me would keep her by my side all night. That's not what I wanted.

"Hey, Mr. Bartender dude—" I called out.

"Oh, God...Cynth. You're so hammered." Cam laughed and shook her head.

He swaggered our way, a white towel slung over one beefy shoulder. He was dark-skinned and muscled, and he wore a devious smirk. He was everything a hot bartender should be.

"Hey," I said, bracing my elbows on the bar. "You want to fuck my friend?"

He was used to this kind of attention from women. Torrance's features registered no shock at my crass interrogation. He knew I wasn't drunk. He'd been fixing me soda and water all night. But I doubted he'd turn down any ploy to get into a girl's pants. He simply smiled and winked at Cameron.

Cam kicked my leg. "I'll never take you drinking again," she said, but her flirtatious smile for the bartender said she wasn't embarrassed in the least. She held up a finger to him. "Give me a second with my girl here."

He shrugged and headed to the register to start closing out.

Cam sighed as she pushed the shot glasses to the edge of the bar. "We only have my car. How are you going to get to your parents'?"

I waved off the issue. "I didn't want to go there anyway."

She hesitated. "Are you going to be okay?"

"Sure," I said, an automatic response.

She swiveled my stool around, forcing me to face her. "I'm serious, Cynth. Today has been..." She trailed off, shaking her head. "Insane."

I'd almost willed all conscious thought of Drew and Chelsea away. But here it was again. Cam's reminder hit like a punch to the throat. My glands thickened, making it hard to swallow. The sour aftertaste of resentment a nauseous sickness churning the pit of my stomach.

What happened wasn't insane. It was very real, and it happened to women all the time. Insanity would've at least freed me of the obligation to *deal* with the fallout. I wished I could just cop out. Skip to the next chapter.

I wasn't that lucky.

I was too aware of my thoughts, and what Drew had done to me.

What Chelsea had done...

I closed my eyes, let the music drown out my thoughts.

"Cynth…" Cam's voice reached out to me. "At least it all went down over spring break. By the time classes resume, everyone will be moved on to the newest scandal."

Except I would not, *could not* move on.

Maybe the board would investigate Drew. His wrist slapped for sleeping with not one but two students, and knocking one of them up. But his parents would buy him out of trouble. Prof. Andrew Abbot would be back to teaching in a month's time. After he married Chelsea, of course, making the whole scandal some romantic tryst.

I would go through my last year as "the other one". The salacious fling and dirty thing.

I didn't have enough money to buy my reputation back.

"Let me get you an Uber."

I opened my eyes. "All right."

Cam took my phone and pulled up the app. "Where do you want to go? The apartment or your parents' house? Honestly?"

The Dock House was much closer to Silver Lake. But our apartment was empty, and would remain so with Cam staying overnight with the bartender.

"I want to go home," I said.

Cam nodded. She knew where I thought home was. "Ride will be here in twenty minutes." She stared down the long bar top at Torrance.

I pushed off the stool and latched on to the counter to gain my balance. I hadn't eaten that day, I realized. "Go ahead. I want to walk down to the dock first. Clear my head. Stare at the stars."

She made an uncertain face, but she was already inching toward her conquest. "You sure?"

I forced a smile. "Yeah. Go on."

She left.

I could take it back. Tell my best friend that no, I don't want to be alone with my thoughts. That it was her idea to stop here and drink away my *insane* problems.

But she was already gone.

I dragged my fingers through my unruly, humidity-tangled hair, and for a second, I felt eyes on me. A creepy feeling of being watched touched the back of my neck, eliciting cold prickles.

I shivered the eeriness away. *I'm distressed. Upset. And alone.*

The lights dimmed, denoting the bar was closed. I slugged toward the boardwalk. All my sad friends had vacated the bar. As I watched Cam leave with the bartender, a desperateness clawed at me from the inside.

What if the bartender had a girlfriend...or a wife? Had she even bothered to ask?

I used to be in the camp that believed men were solely to blame for their cheating ways. Now...? Chelsea's blond hair and perky tits invaded my mind.

God, I loathed her.

My anger toward Cam and even Chelsea was unfounded, I knew that. I was a hypocrite. I had dated my college professor. A cliché deserving of my sad circumstance, as if I had *asked* for it.

Karma.

Maybe I deserved this pain, I thought as I stepped onto the wooden planks of the dock. I wasn't sure why I wanted to walk out there. Maybe it was the dream. My biggest fear had already been realized. I'd already faced the hurt, the pain, that came from discovering the truth.

What else was there to fear?

Yet I wandered onto the pier wishing I could rewrite time—as if just being there was a challenge to fate.

So utterly illogical of me.

Love and pain make us irrational.

I wondered if Drew and Chelsea felt any of this heartache. My mind was going to dark, dark places. Every lecture from my psych classes was spinning in my head. No one ever succeeded in retaliation. And yet…

I wanted retribution.

I wanted both of them to experience this awful, humiliating pain.

Old, water-worn boards creaked beneath my feet. I couldn't tell whether it was the pier swaying or me. I walked to the end of the dock and peered over, into the black water. Lotuses blanketed the inky lake top, their petals a strange iridescent white, dew refracting the light of the stars.

I dropped down, seating myself on the edge. After a while, my phone dinged with a message from the Uber driver. She was in the parking lot. I ignored the message and muted my phone. I didn't care. I curled into a ball right there, the lapping sound of the lake against the boards a soothing calm.

I fell asleep. Or I passed out from hunger, exhaustion. I'm not really sure which. All I know is that I was staring out over the lotuses as the lake breathed them in and out with the rising tide, then…nothing. Blackness blots out that period of time.

There are flashes, glimpses of blood in the water. A red

stained lotus. The crushing pain in my chest as I struggled to breathe. An outline of a man…his hand.

That's all I have now.

Real, recovered, or false memories my mind fabricated to fill the blank.

The next thing I recall is waking up in the hospital.

❧ 10 ❧

DISCOVERY

LAKIN: NOW

The Tiki Hive is just one of the many "tiki" establishments that scatter the Florida coast, and it was the last place of employment for the victim. Unlike other beach bars, with their cheap tiki torch theme, this one is a mix of refined beach life and elegance. A bar for the more affluent residents and tourists of Melbourne.

Sheer white curtains billow in through floor-to-ceiling windows. The scented breeze of ocean and coconut drifts inside, infusing the beachfront restaurant with a lively current of youth.

Mike Rixon was a person of interest further down our list, but Bethany Delany's maternal instinct bumped him up to number one. He was originally questioned due to the flow of drugs around the food and beverage scene. With Joanna's history of drug use, the case detectives already explored this angle, but we can't write anything off; every angle has to be looked at again.

Joanna's toxicology screen was clean of any known street drugs, but that doesn't mean a drug link from her past can be completely ruled out.

Rhys and I are seated across from the restaurant owner at the bar as he dries tumblers. Slowly. Mike Rixon is taking his time, putting us off. He doesn't realize that, with cold cases, he can take his sweet time. We're in no rush. We're the ones who take a fine-tooth comb to the case, going over details that may have been overlooked the first time during a hasty investigation.

After we left the crime scene—*fled*, more accurately— Rhys and I went door-to-door in the neighboring apartment buildings, seeking anyone who might have seen the victim the night of her murder. We turned up nothing. So we decided we'd take a lunch break at the Tiki Hive. Two birds, one stone.

Mike sets a glass down on the matt. "I'm not sure what I can offer you that would help. I told the other guys everything I knew a year ago." He slings a white towel over his shoulder.

Deja vu tickles the edge of my awareness. The action triggers a memory from that night at the Dock House, and Torrance the bartender flashes in my mind. His suave moves. Good looks. The way he winked at Cam.

I push away from the memory and clear my throat. "Let's go over it one last time, anyway."

At his indifferent shrug, I pull out my phone and start recording. While Rhys directs the interview, I try to ignore the sense of familiarity sneaking over me. My heart is a pulse too fast. Palpitations mute my hearing every time Mike smiles.

That smile.

It must be paranoia, the sight of the white lotuses at the crime scene still fresh, but when Mike Rixon looks at me…I swear recognition steals across his sharp features. Something about him feels so familiar.

"She worked that day," Mike confirms with another shrug. "Last I saw of Joanna. I found out two days later she'd been killed when the police showed up here to question me and my staff."

I lift an eyebrow. "Who was questioned?"

He pushes out a long breath. "Me, Sal, Romero, and Jessica."

That doesn't seem like a full staff. I glance around the restaurant floor, noting at least twenty tables.

Rhys catches on. "Do you remember who worked with Joanna during her last shift?"

Mike drives a hand through his wind-tousled hair. "I really don't. I'll go print out the schedule for you, okay?"

"Thank you," I say.

He nods and turns to head to the back, but pauses to add, "Oh, and Torrance." My heart stutters at the name. "He was also here with me that afternoon."

"Wait," I say, stopping him from leaving the bar area. Stalled, I rack my brain for how to press for more information about Torrance. "This person wasn't mentioned in the case file."

Mike shrugs. "Tor wasn't here the day the cops came by."

Rhys studies my profile. I lean closer to the counter, out of his view. "Why not?"

"I don't know. You'll have to ask my brother that himself."

My heart knocks painfully against my chest. *Brother*. "He's here? Now?"

"Yeah. I'll grab him from the back."

Panic flares in my veins, blood rushing. As he pushes through the swing-door, I slide off the stool. I can't be here. If it is the same bartender from the night of my attack, I could compromise the investigation.

Rhys catches my upper arm before I can slip away. "There's more than one Torrance in Florida, Hale. Just like there is more than one lake with lotuses."

"I know." Rhys knows my case as well as I do. He questioned Torrance the bartender. I read the interview he conducted, the probing questions, as he attempted to build a narrative of that night.

The urge to snap the band at my wrist rises up. I tuck a stray hair behind my ear. "I know there are," I say again, "and Torrance's last name isn't Rixon. Mike said *his brother*. So likely, not the same person. But if there's even a slim chance... I need to go."

His mouth curves into a tight frown. If this is the same man from my past, Rhys knows this investigation will change drastically.

"Two women," I say, my voice low. "Both attacked in parallel fashion."

I don't have to say the rest. *One dead. The other not.*

"Rhys, if this is the same person, he might not recognize you. Not if I leave."

But the both of us together will be hard to dismiss.

Rhys nods once. "Go."

I head to the outside deck, my feet heavy, the world at a tilt. My mind is already leaping from connection to connection, linking the two cases together. That's not a good thing. We have to keep them separate to investigate Joanna's murder; it would be a disservice to her to muddy the water before we've even started.

I press my back to a beam underneath the deck canopy, making sure I'm out of eyeshot. Taking even breaths, I slow my heart rate, letting the salty ocean air cleanse my lungs.

I rub the band, twisting it against my skin.

Torrance had a solid alibi for the night of my attack.

Cameron.

But his brother...

I turn and peer around the beam. The kitchen door swings open, and Mike leads his brother toward Rhys. *It's him.* My chest flutters as adrenaline climbs over my nerves.

No one questioned the bartender's brother about the night of my attack. Why would they look at Mike Rixon? There was no feasible reason to interview him, to look at people connected to Torrance.

It's still a stretch to try to link him to the case now, the connection circumstantial, but it's a real thread. The first lead we've ever had in my case.

"Shit," I mutter. *Stop it.*

This is not about me.

I turn away and stare at the beach, repeating that tune: *It's not about me.* I recite it until Rhys is standing in front of me. "Did he recognize you?" I ask.

Suit jacket slung over his shoulder, Rhys rolls up the sleeves of his white dress shirt. "Yeah. I guess most people don't forget being questioned by an FBI agent."

No, most people wouldn't forget that. I shift in place, antsy. Wanting the answers to my questions all at once.

Rhys tics his chin toward the parking lot. Once we're a good distance away from the Tiki Hive, he finally says, "We can't assume anything yet."

Slow breath. "I realize that."

"I'll start by contacting the team at Quantico. We'll get a thorough background check on Mike Rixon and Torrance Carver. Who, apparently, are half siblings, by the way. Let's see where the pieces overlap...if they do at all." He glances my way. "Could be a coincidence."

"There's no such thing."

He huffs a terse breath. "You going to psych one-oh-one me?"

I shrug. "Not psychology, just reason. The very definition of coincidence is two or more events coming together unexpectedly without an obvious explanation." I stop walking so I can face him. "The fact that my case may connect in some way to Joanna's...that's not coincidence. We have two persons of interest linked to two cases. That's fact."

He considers this a moment. "All right. Walk me through a theory."

I look away, past him. "Rhys... I don't have one. I just feel we should investigate—"

"No. You're already hopping to conclusions. I can see it in your eyes. That distant, hopeful look. So let's do this."

I cross my arms. "I take offense to that."

"I don't care. No matter how many cases we work, how many we solve, you're still a victim, Hale. *That* is fact."

His words lance right through me, wounding deep.

He releases a long breath, his features losing their edge. His voice drops to a softer cadence. "I didn't mean it that way." He steps closer, crowding the air with his scent of aquatic cologne. "I just meant that, you come at cases from a victim's point of view. You know what they felt. You can relate to them. That's insight the best case detectives and agents don't have."

"But…?" I provide.

"But, it's not about getting inside the victim's head. We've talked about this. That can be dangerous. You have to know where to draw the line. You have to put hard and cold distance between you and the vic. And I don't think you're going to be able to do that with this particular case."

Stubbornness rears inside me, and I want to scream at him to look at the *facts*. How can he dismiss such an obvious connection? But he's right. God, I hate to admit that, but he is. I'm taking this personally. I'm already too close to it.

From the second I heard Torrance's name mentioned, my mind was already decided. This was about my case, about me. Silver Lake isn't but a hundred miles away. Logically, logistically, it's not out of the realm of possibility that the bartender and his brother could be associated with two similar attacks.

It's unfortunate, but not impossible. Statistically, the brothers are probably associated with other attacks on women in some mundane way. That fact is a terrible reality, though a true one. They work in an environment where alcohol is a factor. That's the cold, hard thinking which will distance me from Joanna's case.

"We're going to look into this," Rhys says, drawing my attention fully on him. "I promise. We're going to investigate every angle and theory, and if—"

"Don't say it." I close my eyes for a beat. "Just don't. I know I leaped. I saw the lotuses at the crime scene…and I was primed to overreact." I swallow hard. "I got this. I'm good."

He nods slowly. "I need you to be objective until it's time not to be."

"All right."

Once we're in the rental car, Rhys hands me my phone. I left it on the bar. "We'll play the interview back at the hotel. I think Rixon might have given us a new lead."

My head buzzes at the news. I'm unsure where I want this new lead to take me—whether it could draw me closer to my killer or not—but at least we haven't hit a dead end yet in the victim's case.

When I dove headfirst into true crime writing, I wanted to be exactly like Rhys. Someone who could think like a criminal, like a killer. Someone who could get inside the perpetrator's head.

I have to be that person now.

We stop for lunch at a burger joint near the hotel, since my dash away from Torrance resulted in no food. In the hotel lobby, I tell Rhys I'm going to my room to freshen up, then I'll meet him at his. I ride the elevator up in a strange kind of trance. Not allowing myself to fully evaluate the events so far.

Once inside my room, I take a quick shower, my thoughts on autopilot. I wrap my hair with a towel and head to my luggage on the bed, noting a folded slip of paper shoved under the door. Assuming it's a bill, I scoop it up and carry it to the room desk, where I can call reception to let them know they made a mistake. I'm not checking out today.

"Hello, yes. I received an invoice—" My words break off as I scan the note.

A roar floods my ears. I can barely hear the woman on the other end of the line trying to get my attention. "Ma'am?"

"Sorry." My voice is unsteady. "I made a mistake." I hang up the receiver. "Oh, God."

I drop the note on the desk, then rush to my bag. I dig out a pair of latex gloves and a forensic baggie. I need to call Rhys.

I stop in the middle of the room. Stalling. Just staring at the letter.

Rhys might not want this case to involve me, but someone else does.

⚜ 11 ⚜

NOTES OF THE PAST

LAKIN: NOW

I *found you.*

How can three simple words incite so much fear?

Out of context, they mean nothing. Like a line from a song. A text message. *I found you* could have infinite meanings.

Amid this cold case, desperately trying to sever myself from the past, these words elicit an image of a man—a memory of a dark silhouette buried in my subconscious. A hand reaching toward the water...

Has he been searching for me the way I've been searching my memories for him?

I've spent the past few years believing this person was my rescuer. But as I stare at the note, unease slips inside me. I recognize the handwriting.

A question I've tried not to ask:

What if the man who snatched me from death is the killer himself?

Cases have been documented. An action taken to end a life, and seconds later, remorse. But that doesn't fit the narrative of the brutal crime. It's hard to paint a scene where a murderer stabs a woman ten times, dumps her in a lake, then returns to save her.

My psychologist said it's likely I conjured this image, this fictitious memory, the same way I imagined the bright, shimmering light.

Chances are, I have no real memory from the time of my death. My mind orchestrated a story to fit the narrative of what I'd been told happened.

Morosely, there is only dark surrounding my death.

But it's in that period of darkness where I find myself lingering. The answer is there…if I can just challenge the fear. Because it's often the unknown people fear the most. When what we dread finally happens, there's nothing to be done but accept the reality of our situation.

That's my utterly logical brain at work. People are remarkably resilient. We recover. Triumph, even. Then wonder why we were scared in the first place.

The impending doom is where fear lives. It thrives in that dark place, like how moss grows on the shaded side of a tree. All that we fear harbors in the shadows. A nameless, faceless monster. That's why, this time, the message has to be brought into the light.

Rhys places the bagged note on the room table. He dusted for prints, but only recovered mine. "The handwriting is characteristically male."

I agree with his analysis. I thought the same. The person who wrote the letter didn't try to hide. Not really— they just didn't give me much else to go on.

Rhys called hotel security to inquire about recorded

hallway footage. The hallway outside my room does have a camera, but the system is down due to security updates.

Perfect timing, or dumb luck?

"If I wanted to frighten someone," Rhys says, "I'd write the most cryptic thing possible. The more information you give a person, the more power you hand them. This note gives nothing away. I think it's meant to scare you."

I lace my fingers together at the base of my neck, elbows resting on my knees. Thinking. "Knowledge is power," I say in agreement. "But then why send a message at all? If I only wanted to frighten someone off a case, there are far more effective ways to do so."

This is the initial theory we've entertained. The author of the note wants us to stop digging into the Delany murder.

The *why* seems obvious enough: the murderer doesn't want to be caught.

The method, on the other hand, is a bit more murky.

"Why target me?" I ask the more apparent question. "If this has nothing to do with before—" *before* feels less threatening than *my murder* "—then why not send you the message? You're the federal agent. It's your call to close the investigation."

I want Rhys to read between the lines. I want him to make the connection.

"I think it's obvious," he says. At my confused expression, he sighs. "Anyone observing us closely—you and me; our team dynamic—can deduce that you're the tool."

"Again," I say, the annoyance tingeing my voice only partially in jest. "So many compliments from you today."

He drives a hand through his hair, looking as agitatedly disheveled as I feel. "Tool as in means to control me."

"Oh." I ponder his theory for a moment, then: "That's rather sexist. You don't believe that, do you?"

Rhys relaxes against the sofa. He swipes his palms along his slacks, smoothing out crease marks. When his gaze lifts to meet mine, I glimpse the faintly concealed worry beneath his guarded eyes.

We've had people try to stymie investigations before. Old, hardboiled detectives who don't want to be proven wrong. Family members suffering guilt, who believe their actions led to the death of their loved ones.

But this is different. This feels sinister.

"I believe that to anyone looking in from the outside, you're a writer on the FBI's payroll. Which means you're important enough to the division to bypass training and lengthy procedures most have to endure to get there. *Important* means you probably have sway." He shrugs against the couch. "Just like Ms. Delany. She looked to you for reassurance. She read your book. She wanted your word that we would solve her daughter's murder."

Fair enough. "That could also make me a target to someone on the inside."

"Like an agent?" he asks, doubt resonating in his tone.

"Why not? If someone got bypassed for a promotion, or didn't make the team... They might blame me for circumventing protocol."

He shakes his head. "No one applies to be in the cold case division." His features darken with his deprecating statement. "What about an obsessed fan?" he challenges with a cock of his head.

I admit, that hadn't occurred. But no—I've hidden my

identity pretty well. "When there are too many possibilities, it's usually the simplest one." I watch him closely.

He smirks. "More psychobabble."

"Philosophy, actually. Occam's razor. Too many assumptions can lead down a wrong path."

"I believe that." He groans as he sits forward to grab my phone. "Regardless, we're doing exactly what the suspect wants. Stalling the investigation."

He moves on, and like being cut free of a noose, tension uncoils within me. Rhys has never brought up my death's door "hallucination." Not once since I confessed it to him. Admittedly, I was anticipating the mention of it at some point—as if the letter could reopen the conversation.

He didn't put credence in my admission then, so I shouldn't expect him to consider the prospect now.

The letter proves nothing.

Rhys may be right about my leaping to conclusions amid this case.

I scrub my hands over my face, trying to rub away the achy tiredness. "Okay. Let's go over the brothers' interview. What did they give us?"

He sets my phone on the table and tabs the Play bar to the middle of the sound bite. "Torrance recalled a line cook that his brother employed for a few weeks. Said he was let go due to some complaints from women."

I quirk an eyebrow. "And this didn't come up during Mike Rixon's first interview with the case detectives?"

"Here. Listen." He starts the recording.

I reach for my notebook. I like to jot down my thoughts as they come to me, transcribe them into the book later. Focusing on the story gives me a degree of separation, too. I need the distraction.

"...We didn't have a full staff that week. Don't you remember, Mike? That guy... What's his name? God, I can't even remember now. Some weird-ass name."

"Kohen."

snap *"That's it. Kohen. He laid out a couple of days that week, and I had to cover his shifts. Worked doubles. Anyway, with all the complaints we got from the women at the bar, Mike fired his ass."*

"What kind of complaints?"

"Some of the regular customers, beach bunnies, we call them. They said he made them uncomfortable. He'd like, just stare at them, all creepy. One woman said he hit on her, offered her free drinks. Ha. Yeah, he had to go."

Rhys pauses the recording.

I look up from my notebook. "Was Torrance able to give a last name for this Kohen who was suspiciously missing from the initial interview with his brother?"

"No," he says. "And even more suspicious is the fact that, according to Rixon, since this guy only worked a few weeks, he didn't bother to log him into the payroll system. Basically, he might not exist."

"Except for in their imagination." A way to throw suspicion off the brothers.

Rhys walks to the wet bar and fetches a bottled water from the mini fridge. His gait is hindered as he puts most of his weight on the leg that didn't suffer a gunshot. After a full day of walking, his leg starts to aggravate him in the evenings.

"But I was able to get the names of the women who

lodged complaints," he says. "Since they frequent the bar, it should be simple enough to track them down."

"Maybe," I say, "if they're at the bar often enough, they can even confirm whether or not the brothers were actually working the night of Joanna's murder." Because otherwise, we'll have to pry that information out of the staff. Family members cover for each other.

A smile twitches at my lips, thinking about Rhys fighting off the advances of the beach bunnies. "You should take the lead on that. I'm sure the beach bunnies will take to you."

He takes a swig of water and recaps the bottle. "Funny. But I do have a way with the ladies, don't I?"

I crane an eyebrow. "Is that a joke, Agent Nolan?"

"Don't get used to it."

I shake my head, then start on my notes again. I'm sure Rhys is trying to lighten the mood, and I appreciate his attempt at humor, for my sake. I halt writing as a thought occurs.

I eye my phone, wondering what Torrance the bartender said about me. It's not as if we're friends, or remotely close; brought together by unfortunate circumstance. After that night, according to Cameron, she never saw her spring break fling again. A one-night stand that, after her best friend was attacked and nearly died, she forgot all about.

Then the interview when Rhys reopened my case. A ten-minute conversation with Torrance that only reiterated what I already knew. I walked off toward the dock. Torrance and Cam left the bar and went to his apartment. Nothing else.

I reach for my phone. I need to know what he said

about Joanna and me. It's too uncanny that two women were attacked in establishments where he worked.

I try to picture Mike Rixon's face coming toward me on the dock…

Did Torrance's brother come there looking for him, only to find me? Are Joanna and I trying to tell the same story?

"I think I got enough for now," I say as I stand, tucking my notebook close to my chest. I slip my phone into my back pocket. "I'm calling it a day. See you in the morning."

"We should share a room."

His words stop me at the door. "Are you serious? Because of the cryptic, three-word note? I thought you said we shouldn't take it seriously."

"I never said that. Be it an obsessed fan, jealous agent, or unhinged ghost from your past, I err on the side of caution."

His mention of a ghost from my past makes me shiver. He hasn't forgotten. Does that mean he believes it's a possibility, or just that he believes I think it's real?

"And your tingly agent senses tell you I'm not exactly safe," is all I say.

"They tell me that this person knows where you're staying. They know your room number, because they most likely followed you here." He pauses to let this sink in. "Until we smoke out the author of the note, I'm keeping you close. You're staying in my room tonight."

12

BOOK OF CAMERON

LAKIN: THEN

Awakening in a hospital room is like being born a second time, only with complete awareness. Senses are overstimulated. Lights are too bright. Noises are too loud. Smells are overpowering. Starchy sheets rub against skin like saltwater abrading a wound.

Every move triggers discomfort. You have no memory of what hunger feels like.

Only thirst.

My mouth was so parched, I can still recall the scratchy feel of sandpaper on my tongue. Like spider webs at times. I kept trying to pull the webbing out of my mouth, until one of the nurses reduced the morphine drip.

Then…the pain.

My body was a lightning rod for pain.

It took a week for me to remember my name.

It took another two weeks for me to be able to use the bathroom on my own.

The first time I saw the mutilation to my body in the bathroom mirror…

Let's just say, the physical agony was bearable compared to the psychological trauma.

But the worst part was the isolation. It was worse than what I suffered after Amber. I'd never felt so alone, so cutoff from the world. It was as if my own small world had slammed to a halt, and everyone else kept going without me. I was stuck in limbo.

I spent the first days drifting in and out of sleep, healing, recovering. My body fighting to live. My mind hadn't yet grasped why I was in the hospital. I was existing on a plane somewhere between consciousness and a nightmare. Struggling to fully wake up, like a perpetual state of sleep paralysis.

When I fought my way to the land of the living, Detective Dutton was the first person my blurry gaze latched on to.

My first impression of Detective Dutton:

Fat and lazy. With a protruding belly that flopped over his black duty belt, he appeared to me the very essence of what was wrong with the world, America in particular. Do just enough to say you're doing your job, but don't strive for anything greater.

God forbid he actually listened. I don't think Dutton believed me, or he didn't care enough to find my killer. For him, the threat was gone…if it ever existed in the first place. I could tell by the way his watery, cataract eyes scrutinized me; he was from the old boys' club—the one that thinks women get what's coming to them if they don't behave.

Per procedure, Dutton brought in the doctor to check

my vitals and run tests before I was permitted to speak with him. Then he dove straight into questioning.

"Do you remember being at the Dock House?"

"Do you recall who was there that night? Who did you talk to…see?"

"Can you remember anything at all?"

My answer to every question: *I don't remember*.

This incensed the detective. He was anxious to put the case to bed, and I couldn't help his case. But I was in disbelief. As he revealed what was known about the night of my attack, it was as if he was relaying a story about someone else.

He rushed through his speculated theory about what happened:

Cameron and I went to the Dock House. Drew, still enraged from our fight, tracked me to the bar and cornered me on the dock after closing. We fought, and he stabbed me ten times, then tried to hide the evidence by disposing of my body in Dead River. The dark irony of the river's name was not lost on me. Only nothing but alligators move in Dead River (which, according to Dutton, I was lucky 'not to be eaten by a gator'). So a rare current must have swept me closer to Lake Eustis, where I washed up onto the lake's shore and, hours later, was discovered by an early morning fisherman. I was nonresponsive by the time paramedics arrived, presumed dead.

But they revived me.

I had a pulse, although faint. I had lost a lot of blood. I was rushed to Silver Lake Memorial.

"It's been eight days," Detective Dutton stressed. "It's critical that you try, Cynthia. Try to remember what happened that night. Do you recall seeing Drew at the bar?"

I had no memory of the things Dutton revealed. My heart rate spiked, the beeping of the heart monitor increased. A deep ache bloomed beneath the sharp, physical pain, and I struggled to breathe. *It's not true.* Only somewhere hidden in my subconscious the truth was surfacing. I felt the familiar sickness in my soul; the twisting blade of betrayal.

Chelsea was pregnant.

I fought with Drew.

Cameron and I went to the Dock House.

And then...

I shook my head. "I don't remember." Pain lanced my brain; a rift, a fault forming a divide.

Dutton frowned. "According to your friend Cameron, you walked down to the pier. Do you remember who else was there? Did you see Drew?"

The mention of Cam sparked a flicker of memory. For some reason, hearing my best friend's name triggered anger. I was upset with her...but I didn't know why.

"I want to see her," I said, my throat raw.

The detective crossed his arms, moved close to my bedside. "Don't you want to see your parents first?" he asked. "They've been worried sick."

Right. My parents. "Yes, please send them in," I said. "I don't want to talk about this anymore."

I was fuzzy from the morphine, and generally discombobulated from what my body had suffered, but I could still discern the way Detective Dutton looked at me, the judgmental gleam in his narrowed eyes. He analyzed me like a suspect.

"All right," he said. "We'll pick this up again once you've had time to recover more. Please reach out to me if you do remember anything at all…no matter how trivial. Maybe you'll start to get your memory back when the drugs wear off." He laid his card on the tray and tapped it twice.

We both knew that wasn't true. The first hours of any investigation were imperative to find the perpetrator. As such, the first recollections from a victim are vital. Chances were, any recovered memories would be suspect to media influence, and what my family and friends revealed to me. The narrative of my attack would be lost until my mind decided otherwise.

I found the strength to push myself up on the bed as my parents entered the room. Seeing my mother's face in that moment… It was like a blow to my shredded stomach. She had aged ten years since I last saw her, and my father —the ever stubborn, unmovable rock in our small family —was a withered shell of his former self.

I bore the hugs, the touches, the fretting over my comfort, only because they didn't probe or demand to know what happened. Their relief over their only daughter being brought back from the dead was their sole focus, their moment of rejoice. They didn't want to taint the reunion. I was grateful.

Once I convinced them I needed rest, stating I was exhausted but wanted to see Cam, they brought her in and reassured me they'd be right across the hallway.

At first, she wouldn't look at me. Cam cast her gaze at the room floor. "I'm so relieved, Cynth. You have no idea how worried I—"

"What happened?"

She looked at me then. And I could see it in her eyes. Guilt. She moved closer and took a deep breath, bracing herself. "You were so distraught," she said. "I tried to get you to leave with us…"

"Who is *us*?" I demanded. I still wasn't sure why I felt so hostile toward her.

She crossed her arms, defensive. "Torrance. The bartender. Remember? You told me to go home with him. I mean, you practically pimped me out to him."

I rested my head against the pillow. "I don't remember, Cam. Shit, I don't remember anything about that night."

The expression on her face morphed. It was completely out of place, but for some strange reason, one of Drew's lectures came back to me. The one where he discussed perception. How there was no way to prove alternate dimensions existed, but that there were alternate worlds, if only because of perception. Seven billion different alternate worlds, to be exact. Because there were seven billion people, all seeing the world through their own eyes.

Cam stared at me through the lens of how she viewed me in her world. I was some possible complication to her life had I been able to remember. I knew this, because the sudden relief that washed over her face revealed that truth.

She stepped closer and rested her hand on my arm, ignoring the tubes, the tape. The bruises and cuts. "Cynthia, I don't know what to say. I'm sorry. We got drunk. We were both so wasted. I tried to get you to leave with me, but you were obstinate—you wanted to stay. Nothing I said convinced you otherwise. So I got you an Uber. I knew your ride was only minutes away. I don't know what happened."

Her answer felt wrong; it felt rehearsed. I'm sure she'd

given Detective Dutton this story over and over. But I was her friend. I had been attacked and left for dead. I *had* died. Dumped like garbage in a lake.

A blurry image crept over me. The first glimpse of him reaching toward me through the shimmering ripples…

I sealed my eyes closed.

"What was I so angry about, then?" I asked, forcing my eyes open and the image away. "What did I do…what did I say? Tell me, Cam."

Nervously, she glanced toward the door. Then: "Don't you remember?"

Looking to the one window in my room, I fought hard to keep the tears of frustration from filling my eyes, but I was frightened. Someone had tried to *kill* me—that fact was finally sinking in. Up until that moment it felt too surreal, too foreign, to be true.

"How did this happen to me?" My words stuttered out on a weak, shaky breath.

Cam removed her hand from my forearm and clasped my fingers. "You were so upset, Cynth. It scared me," she said, and I swung my gaze to meet hers. "You were still so upset over Drew and Chelsea, and the baby…" She raised her eyebrows.

I gripped her hand tighter. "Was Drew there?"

Her features fell. "No, he wasn't, but…" She trailed off, swallowed.

"What, Cam?"

A tear escaped the corner of her eye. "It's my fault. God, I shouldn't have left you. It's all my fault."

"It's not your fault." I tried to console her.

She shook her head. "Yes, it is. I can't do this. I have to go."

Cam swiped hard at the tears trailing her cheeks before she turned away, heading toward the door.

"He has to pay…"

Her words floated to my ears, a muffled whisper choked by her sobs.

13

GHOSTS

LAKIN: NOW

My fingers stall over the laptop keyboard. My hands are trembling.

Where did that come from?

I never remembered Cam saying that to me in the hospital before.

He has to pay.

"It's not real," I say out loud, so I can reiterate it, so I can believe it.

Memories are tangling. I'm filling in blanks. A writer tends to do that—to create the best story possible in place of fact.

I delete the page and yank the USB drive from my laptop, then clip it to the fob on my key ring. I don't want to read that passage again.

Then I do something I'm ashamed of, but that I've done too many times before. I pull up my Facebook app and type Cam's name into the search.

The deeply buried psychologist in me detests social media. That's why I don't have a personal account. I have one for my pen name that I only use to cross post to my author page when my publisher needs me to update fans.

For thousands of years, people have lived without documenting their daily lives. I wonder how the younger generations will fair later in life with a constant reminder of every single day of their existence. When the pop-up pic displays, showing each day with a happy memory— because most people only post the happy ones. Not the truth.

The pic taken with the bestie in front of a wine bar, all smiles, was also the day that you discovered your boyfriend sleeping with another woman. Or the day your parent died. Or the day you railed on a coworker, saying horrible things. Or the day you did some despicable thing that you'd rather forget...

But your timeline won't let you.

Humans were designed to forget. Our brains are not meant to retain every day of our lives. It's the only way we can come to terms with and reconcile our past; accept the life we've lived.

The brain as a whole compared to a computer is supposed to have faulty memory chips. That's how we're able to move on.

I scroll through the profiles until I find her. I knew Cam moved to West Melbourne a while ago, but...

A breath lodges in my throat, strangled at the base of my neck. I force myself to breathe past the constriction.

Cameron's most recent post shows her engaged in a loving embrace with her husband, Elton, his arms wrapped around her swollen belly. The post proudly states: *We're pregnant!*

I stare at her smile, perfect, bright, and wonder what worries lurk behind her happy image, if it's a facade. What memory will Cam recall when this pic resurfaces a year from now?

I close the app and set my laptop and phone aside on the sofa. Rhys is still down at the hotel coffee shop, so I indulge in the few minutes I have alone. I head to the bathroom, where I stand before the full-length mirror. I place my hands over my stomach, the pads of my fingers instinctually connecting with the beveled scars beneath my shirt.

Ten stab wounds. One deep laceration. Overkill is the term Detective Dutton used. It only takes one perfectly placed knife to the heart to kill...and yet my attacker didn't go for the kill.

They went for pain.

Majority of the wounds were inflicted to my abdomen. During the many operations to keep my newly revived life afloat, my uterus and ovaries were removed, along with part of my intestinal track. *Damaged beyond repair*, is what the surgeon had told me when I became conscious.

I allow myself one moment to feel the pain, then drop my hands.

In college, I had proclaimed that I didn't want kids. Like many young women, I had no real clue what I wanted. But to have the decision made for me...to be stripped of the chance...the choice...

That's a wound that will never heal.

The room door opens, and I cross to the sink and turn on the tap. Cold water flows over my heated palms. I splash my face, waking myself from the past, chasing the bitter nausea away.

"You get enough writing in?" Rhys asks from the room.

"I did. Thanks." I find it difficult to write around others. Rhys knows I'm easily distracted and do my best work alone, and though not easily swayed, he agreed to give me half an hour to myself in compromise to my sharing his room.

I should've used that time to work on Joanna's story. Instead, some needy part of me craved to open my book. Maybe it was the fact that Joanna didn't have many friends that made me desire to revisit Cam, to dissect that moment between us in my hospital room.

He has to pay.

A chill touches the back of my neck, and I rub it away. I have to stop relating to the victim. Cam was upset. If the memory is real, then of course she was angry with Drew in that moment. I was hurt and angry myself. That's the reason we went to the Dock House in the first place.

Nothing ever came of Cam's proclamation.

We all moved on.

I close my eyes, and hear Rhys move closer to the bathroom. "I was thinking about contacting Ms. Delany again to see if the vic kept up with anyone from her previous life."

When I open my eyes, I see his reflection in the mirror. Shirt rolled up over his forearms, he leans against the doorjamb, paper cup outstretched toward me.

"I was actually just thinking the same thing." I turn and accept the cup of tea. "Thanks."

He nods in acknowledgement.

"She tried to sever herself from that lifestyle," I say, cupping the warmth against my palms. "That meant severing friendships. People who still used drugs. But maybe there was at least one person she kept in contact with, someone she just couldn't let go of."

Cam's happy, smiling face flashes before my vision.

"That's what I'm hoping for," he says, then takes a sip of his coffee. "We need at least one person who she confided in. Someone who she told her secrets and worries to."

I slip past him into the room. "Who do you confide in?"

"My cleaning lady," he quips.

I smile and set my cup on the nightstand beside the bed nearest the window. "You're not even joking, are you?"

"Not in the least." He unbuttons his dress shirt. "She's a great listener."

I watch Rhys pull off his shirt, revealing a white T-shirt beneath. He's defined; tight, sinewy muscle makes up his flawlessly formed physique. He folds his dress shirt and lays it and his neatly folded slacks at the end of his bed. He's the epitome of a federal agent. Organized, well mannered, loyal. And yet the scattering of scars covering his arms hint to the turbulence just beneath that veneer.

He's a sidelined field agent. Damaged goods. He has the aches and pains that come with the job, but he no longer has the job he was born to do.

I wish I could've met him before his injury, before he was sanctioned to the cold case division. Who was Rhys Nolan then? A more vibrant version of the faded and distant man I see now?

We have that in common, too, I guess. We don't share

much, but we have that—that panging, niggling reminder of who we once were. A cruel souvenir with every glimpse in the mirror. It leaves a bitter aftertaste in your mouth.

Rhys and I, we have our bitterness.

He tugs back the blankets, props the pillows against the headboard. "While conducting the rest of the interviews, we can get handwriting samples," he says.

The mattress beneath me feels wooden, unforgiving. "I'm in your room, and now you want handwriting samples to compare to the note." I cock my head as I study his backside. His shoulders tense. "Can I ask you something, and you give me an honest answer?"

Once he finally has the bed made to his liking, Rhys climbs in and looks at me. "Yes."

I nod, inhaling a quick breath. "Are you actually concerned about the author of that note, or is this fishing expedition an excuse to hunt down a suspect in the field?"

He doesn't respond right away. Instead, he throws back the covers and, planting his feet on the floor, he keeps me in his sights as he stands and crosses the small span between us. I have to angle my head back to meet his eyes as he towers over me.

"Honestly," he says, voice gravelly low, the question implied.

I swallow. "Yes."

"I'm always going to protect," he says. "That comes first. Before the case, before the evidence…it's how I'm wired. And no matter how bruised and beaten my ego gets, my pride doesn't factor in. Ever."

"All right," I say, still holding his steely gaze.

He reaches over and clicks off the lamp. "Goodnight, Hale."

The room morphs into darkness, for which I'm thankful. I don't want him to see the shame I know registers on my face. "Night, Rhys."

I sink farther beneath the cool sheets, listening to the hum of the air conditioner, acutely aware of the note's proximity to me.

Where is the author of the note now? How close are they to me?

I grab my phone from the nightstand and plug in my earbuds. I replayed the audio file of Torrance's interview three times, listening for the exact moment he realized that I was a part of the investigation. I listen to it again, trying to merge the past with the present, to discern if Torrance and his brother know more than they claim.

Rhys wants handwriting samples—and he's looking for the suspect amid Joanna's case. He still refuses to see the emerging pattern, the lotus petals floating on the lake...

If I mark today as the nexus where my and the victim's paths crossed, then I might know where to start.

❧ 14 ❧

BOOK OF HIM

LAKIN: THEN

I read his letter in the sun.

It wasn't some cliché rainy night, with howling wind and creaking shutters banging against the house. It was a bright, sunny morning when I held the off-white stationary in my hands as I stared out over Silver Lake from my parents' back porch. I remember thinking the paper was so creamy. Soft and rich. Delicate. And the morning was so bright.

Once I was released from the hospital, I returned to my parents' home to continue my physical therapy. I took the semester off from college. That choice was made more for self-preservation than for my recovery. The investigation had circled heavily around Drew. Detective Dutton liked him for the prime suspect, and the media smelled rich blood in the water.

I was in hiding, more or less. Wary of the sharks in the water.

A few letters and emails came at first. Prayers. Well wishes for my recovery. The hope that my attacker would be arrested.

Then others started to pour in.

Angry, spiteful letters written anonymously, blaming me for my own mishap. I had been drunk, at a bar, therefore I was asking for trouble. I had never corrected Detective Dutton on my assumed state at the Dock House. Even if I'd tried, I doubted he would've believed me. The letters asked the question: What right did I have to point the finger at Andrew Abbot? A wealthy, well respected member of an affluent family.

And as I predicted, to stave off the negative media frenzy, Drew and Chelsea announced their engagement the same week I was released from the hospital. It momentarily thwarted the investigation, but Detective Dutton used the announcement to his advantage, singling out a motive for Drew.

Then the media turned on me. I was painted as the eyesore, the irritating blemish in Drew's picturesque life. The scorned, jealous, obsessive student with an unhealthy obsession for her college professor. I read it all in the letters. I was called names: whore, slut, even prostitute. One of the anonymous letters declared I had been trying to blackmail Drew into giving me passing grades.

It became a wild, swirling vortex, and when Drew was ultimately cleared with an alibi, I knew the dam was about to burst, the floodwaters coming for me.

My mother tried to get me to focus on recovery. Cam tried to reassure me that it would pass—like every drama at school, people would soon move on, forget about the scandal.

But I was being sucked down by the undertow.

Then *his* letter arrived.

Just when the storm clouds seemed to be dispersing, the clear blue day giving me hope, chance guided my hand to pluck his letter from the pile. I sat on the rocking chair on my mother's porch and tore open the envelope, and a shiver rocked me.

I've never seen anything as beautiful as you.

The horror in your face, the pale wash of your porcelain skin, as the darkest red swathed you in a shroud of death.

Mesmerizing.

You're everything I have been searching for.

Do your wounds ache with the memory of the blade?

Do you feel that hollow echo longing for completeness each time you touch the scars?

I have to know the answers.

We have to meet.

Blood roared in my ears, my heartbeat erratic, mounting higher. Tremors shook the letter from my hands. I pressed my palm to my chest, inhaled deeply, trying to control the climbing panic.

I hyperventilated until I shut down, blacked out. My body's response to the flood of adrenaline. Its own defense mechanism since the attack. I just turned off.

No one discovered me in that state, which I was thankful. My mother had been through enough. When I came to, I had balled the letter in my fist. I clutched it tighter, attempting to crush it into nonexistence.

Even now, I don't fully understand my response to the message. It was vague, cryptic, and no actual threat was made in those blocky letters, but the veiled warning rung clear.

It could've came from some deranged person. A sick individual that just wanted a connection to a crime. When I became involved in true crime writing, I learned there were a lot of people like that, obsessively following crime stories.

Or it could've came from the killer himself.

Or the person who pulled me from the water.

I analyzed the note, the words, trying to decipher the meaning. Whoever sent the letter, it didn't matter. I realized that I didn't only have my killer to fear—there were other disturbed, unhinged people in the world that wanted me dead.

In the end, only one action could be taken in response.

My killer had no face. Fear is a living, breathing entity when you're staring into the unknown. When you don't know who is your friend and who is an enemy. Any choice, any direction, and I could collide into the wrong person.

I packed a bag that night and boarded a bus.

I left Florida. I took the money I had in my college savings, and I pulled up a map on my phone and chose the most obscure place I could find. Then I promised myself that I wouldn't run forever. I swore that I would catalog the events, the details, everything the police were overlooking in connection to my attack, and I would solve my own murder.

And I did that with a vehement hunger for six months before my case ground to a halt, the leads dried up, and it went cold.

It would be years before I returned to Silver Lake.

⚜ 15 ⚜

CHARGE IN THE AIR

LAKIN: NOW

A storm hovers on the edge of Melbourne. The sky over Melbourne Beach swirls in striations of grays and purples, as if an angry hand swiped the sky. Bruised clouds roll over the rising deep-blue waves. It's beautiful and violent, a turbulent dance. A kind of promise lingers in the air. How the waves reach toward the sky, the crest kissing the sand like an angry lover, trying to fuse a connection. But the sand keeps receding.

The packed grains beneath my bare feet corrode with the outgoing tide. Captured by its lover, after all.

I remind myself that this is only my perception. Hundreds of skin-clad bodies dot the beach, viewing the doused sun as a cool reprieve from the heat. Rhys and I stand out amid the beach goers in our slacks and pressed shirts. Anyone trying to avoid the cops can make us a mile away.

He walks along the hard-packed sand while I choose to

get my feet wet. We're returning to the Tiki Hive, but this time we're here to talk to the beach bunnies. They're not difficult to locate. Three women in their late-fifties with skin the color of tawny leather, the texture just as coarse.

"Yikes," Rhys comments, and I laugh despite myself.

"That's Florida for you," I say. "No fear of the sun." I don't think my mother knew what sunscreen was when I was a child. I have a spattering of freckles across the bridge of my nose to prove it.

Rhys lifts his shades for a second to get a better gawk at the women. "Least you don't take if for granted. I can count the number of days I saw the sun in my childhood. When it did peek out, we got the day off of school."

I glance at him. "You're joking."

"Seriously. Other kids got snow days. I got sun days." He gives me a wink.

I don't know whether or not to believe him, but I appreciate his effort to keep the mood light. Our first day here met with a rocky start. I can trust his opinion on the lotuses; Florida is a haven to the white lilies. Maybe somebody did plant them there in memory of Joanna—*not* the killer—but a friend, or a family member.

I'm having a more challenging time buying into the theory that Torrance's connection to Joanna's murder is only a coincidence. And the note…slipped under my room door, meant to frighten me away… That can only be intentional. But with only three words to go on, after sleeping on the matter, I'm no longer certain the author is the same person who penned the cryptic note after my attack.

Still, fresh start.

Today we search for the elusive Kohen. We'll either

get answers, or hit a wall. Either way, that item on the checklist gets marked off so we can move on to the next bullet point.

Rhys and I have a system, and it hasn't failed us yet.

We were able to interview Jamison Smith—the boyfriend—over the phone this morning. He's out of town on business. Jamison reiterated the same thing he told Detective Vale a year ago. With a little less detail.

This is normal, and bodes well for checking him off our list. Liars tend to elaborate, adding more and more layers to pad their story over time.

The loose sand sticks to my feet as we approach the sunning ladies stretched out on beach chairs just steps from the Tiki Hive's deck. I set my phone to Record inside my bag. The wind could disrupt the feed, so this way we might get clear statements.

Rhys flashes his badge. "Morning, ladies. I'm Special Agent Rhys Nolan. Could we have a quick word?"

One of the weathered-looking women smiles up at Rhys. "Just a quickie, special agent? I'd like to think we could make it last a bit longer than that." She elbows her friend to her right, and I swear I see a flush crawl up the back of Rhys's neck.

The other woman sits forward and shields her eyes as the sun peeks out. "Why do they call y'all special, anyway? That's what I'd like to know. Got a special package you carry around, do ya?"

Christ. They have no shame. I eye the mimosas next to their chairs. "State law prohibits alcohol on the beach."

The third woman noticeably rolls her eyes. "Hon, ain't nobody caring about that." She looks to her friends.

"Seems this one might have a thing for the agent, here. Maybe we should play nice."

Now I'm the one blushing. My fingers seek the comforting feel of the rubber band against my skin.

Rhys clears his throat and directs the conversation back on topic. "The owner of the Tiki Hive mentioned you might know how we can locate a man named Kohen."

"Vivian," the first lady says. "But you can call me Vinnie. And why do you want to know about him for? Lord, that boy was something else."

Rhys cranes an eyebrow. "Meaning what, exactly, Ms. Vinnie?"

She snorts. "Haven't been a miss in ages, but thank you, Agent Nolan." She reaches for her drink. "Kohen was sure nice to look at, but he had this way about him." She visibly shivers. "Something just seemed off, you know what I mean?"

It's difficult to read vague statements. People interpret interactions differently, in their own understanding of the world. "He made you uncomfortable," I say, offering clarity.

Vinnie nods. "Oh, did he ever. I mean, don't get me wrong. I was flattered a young thing like him was interested, but my warning bell was going off. I have years of experience, and I've learned to trust my instincts when it comes to men."

The other two women nod enthusiastically, offering words of agreement.

"Did Kohen do something in particular to sound your alarm?" Rhys asks.

The woman seated in the middle responds. "This one time, we were up at the bar, and he showed me a picture he had on his phone of this girl all tied up in ropes. Said that's what he'd like to do to me. Can you imagine?"

I trade a glance with Rhys. "Was this image of someone he knew, or was it from the Internet?" I ask.

The woman shakes her head. "I have no idea. I didn't ask. I laughed it off as a ludicrous idea, and two days later Mike had fired him, anyway."

I make a mental note on the timeline. "And your name?"

She smiles. "Angela Moretti." She spells it out, and then states all their names for the record. "I suppose this is being recorded, too? You being the government and all."

By law, I have to make them aware. "Yes. I'm recording our conversation, though it's not for government use. It's for my personal notes."

Angela huffs a derisive laugh. "Sure, honey."

The wind picks up, and Rhys turns his back to shelter us from the sand spray. "We appreciate your honesty and cooperation. Did any of you ladies ever see Kohen and Joanna Delany together?"

"Oh…" Vinnie grins knowingly. "So that's what this is all about. That poor girl. So tragic. Such a horrible way to die." She shakes her head. "And her mother, dear lord. Poor thing. But to answer your question, no. Not to my recollection. Kohen wasn't an outgoing sort; you had to draw him out of his shell. And, well, Joanna was out of his league. That would've never happened."

Rhys cocks his head. "But he mentioned her before?"

Angela frowns. "She was a very beautiful girl, agent. Of course he noticed her. All the men at the bar did." She glances at her friends. "She was once this big model, I heard."

"Do you know where Kohen is now?" I ask.

Vinnie hesitates, and Angela notices. "Oh, you old hussie."

"What? A cougar's got to eat. Shoot." Vinnie looks up at us. "It was just the one time, but he took me back to his place." She gives us the address and directions.

Angela *hmphs*. "Sounds like you've been there more than once."

I speak up. "Can any of you ladies recall seeing either Mike or Torrance working the night of March twenty-third?"

"The night Joanna died, you mean?" Vinnie says. I nod. "I'm sorry, hon. I can't say for sure. Too many mimosas, and too many of the same kind of days all run together." The other women agree to this.

"Well, thank you, ladies." Rhys interrupts before they can derail the conversation again. "I believe that's all we need at this time. We appreciate your cooperation. The government extends its gratitude, also."

We start off, but Vinnie catches my pant leg, letting Rhys get a few steps ahead. "Little advice, darling. That one there is a bundle of sexual tension just waiting to erupt. You take care of that man before he blows. Boy, I'd love to be the one to release the pressure on that steamy kettle."

The women nod in agreement, and a warm flush prickles my cheeks. "Thanks. I'll keep that in mind."

I'm able to pry myself away from the beach bunnies before they can start in on my lack of love life. I have a feeling that was next on their agenda. When I catch up to Rhys, I notice his slight limp as he navigates the boardwalk.

I slip on my shoes. "Is the sand bothering your leg?"

He noticeably corrects his gait. "Not too bad. It's a good workout, though. I just need to strengthen the muscles." Then he switches the topic. "What else did the beach bunnies have to say?"

I reach into my bag and dig out my phone to stop the recorder. "Nothing relevant."

He glances back at me, but says nothing. I can see it in his steel-gray eyes, though. He somehow knows. "How do you do that?" I ask.

He walks ahead. "Do what?"

"Nothing," I say, because he knows exactly what I mean, and he'll only deny it. I may have knowledge and skilled insight into people due to my years devoted to study, but he was born with an inherent intuition. I admit that it makes me jealous.

As we merge onto the pavement of the beach parking lot, I ease up beside him. "You only dismiss psychology because you don't need it to do your job," I say. "You read people naturally."

He clicks the key fob to unlock the sedan. "I don't dismiss it. I just think there's more than that to people. And you have to use it all to work a case."

I stare at him for a moment. "I agree. But since I don't possess that natural ability—"

"You do," he says, then turns to look at me. "Just learn to trust it."

I hold his gaze, wondering what he sees that I don't when I look in the mirror. His phone rings, the interruption allowing me out of a critical self-analysis.

"Markus, what do have?" Rhys holds his phone to his ear as he stares out over the sand dunes. "Okay, thanks. Go ahead and forward the reports to me." He ends the call. "Background checks on Mike and Torrance came back. I had Markus dig deeper into Torrance this time around."

Torrance wasn't a suspect or even much of a person of interest when we were working my case. His alibi was solid. "Anything come up?"

His shoulders deflate. "Nothing much. A few bad checks on Mike's part. Some past due payments to venders."

I frown. "And Torrance?"

He pockets his phone. "One expunged assault record. Victim was a sixteen-year old girl." He heads toward the car and opens the driver-side door. "You can read me the file on our way to Kohen's place."

Expunged could mean the charge was sealed because he was a minor at the time.

Rhys leans in and says, "Stay here. I'll be right back."

He closes the door and takes off at a jog before I can ask where he's going. I watch him push through the entrance of the Tiki Hive. I tap my foot as I wait, becoming impatient, but then I see him exit the restaurant.

"What was that about?" I ask as he climbs in behind the wheel.

He hands me a baggie. "Writing samples. Mike and Torrance discard their orders and cash receipts in the trashcan behind the bar."

Which means he didn't need a warrant to obtain them. I quickly glance over the handwriting on the tabs. "It doesn't look similar."

"We'll send it on to the team. Get analysis. Whoever wrote the note might've attempted to disguise their handwriting."

I let this sink in, thinking. I still remember in vivid clarity the note that was sent to my parents' house. The blocky letters, the words. The note pushed under my hotel room door was a close enough match.

Logically, neither Mike nor Torrance had reason to frighten me years ago during the investigation. They weren't suspects. Still, after years of questioning the motive behind the letter, I discerned the author could be delusional, or suffer from some form of erotomania.

If either one of the brothers exhibits this behavioral trait then maybe I'm not seeing the bigger picture.

"This is good, Rhys. Thorough." If for no other reason than to check the brothers off *my* list.

❦ 16 ❦

IMPULSE CONTROL

LAKIN: NOW

Parked two blocks down from Kohen's house, Rhys uses his database to do a quick search on our suspect. Here's what we know about the former Tiki Hive waiter:

His full name is Kohen Louis Hayes. Twenty-five. White. Male. Single. He lived with his mother, Jennifer Hayes (never married) up until a year and a half ago, when he rented a small suburban house off the A1A. He has no credit cards. He attended a community college for computer science for a few months, then dropped out to pursue a scattering of food and beverage jobs.

Kohen does have one offense. At the age of nineteen, he was in a bar altercation that resulted in the police locking him up for a night. He was released the next day on his own recognizance. The other participant in the fight never pressed charges.

Most young men have a lack of impulse control at that

age—yet, was this a one-time occurrence, or a marker for the onset of a disturbing behavioral pattern?

On paper, nothing out of the ordinary stands out. He appears to have little ambition, but he did move out of his mother's house, which is no small feat for most young males today. But the question is, for someone who appears to be comfortable coasting through life, what prompted this sudden surge of independence? What spurred him to attend college in the first place?

Typically, the answer is pretty commonplace: a woman.

This could also be a likely reason for the altercation.

That would be the natural, healthy reason. There are, of course, the less common and more disturbing motives: drug use; illicit fetishes; other various illegal activities— all of which privacy would be a necessity.

I'll deduce more once we interview him.

Rhys does a quick periphery check around the house, making sure there are no attack dogs or other threats, before we approach the one-story home. It's an off-white, eggshell color, darkened by age and neglect. The porch sinks in toward the middle, boards creak beneath our feet.

Rhys knocks.

There's a noise behind the door, like someone was already watching us from the peephole. Rhys's hand goes to his gun harness, palm hovering over his service piece as a precaution. After a reasonable amount of time, the door opens. I recognize Kohen from the description the beach bunnies gave us.

"Kohen Hayes?" Rhys addresses him as an inquiry. He says it's best to start an introduction with a question, to get the suspect used to answering questions right from the start.

As Kohen's hands are in view and he doesn't appear to be a threat, Rhys bypasses his weapon and takes out his ID.

Kohen's dark eyebrows draw together in a confused countenance. "That's me," he says. "What do you want?"

I can see why he had a bit of sway over the ladies. Despite his young age, Kohen is strikingly handsome and carries himself with assured confidence. His shoulders pull back, bringing him to a level height with Rhys.

Rhys makes the introductions, then says, "Mr. Hayes, we have a few questions we need answered pertaining to Joanna Delany." He gets right to the matter, testing Kohen's reaction to the victim's name.

With only the slightest thinning of his lips, Kohen steps onto the porch and shuts the door behind him, otherwise stoic. He stuffs his hands into his jean pockets and lifts his chin. His way of stating he'll talk to us, for now.

"When was the last time you recall seeing Ms. Delany?" Rhys asks.

A shrug. "I worked a shift with Jo the day she was killed," he answers honestly, and with very little emotive tone. He also refers to the victim by a familiar nickname, denoting he knew her better than a coworker or acquaintance.

"Do you remember about what time she left work that evening?" Rhys continues the questioning.

Kohen's deep-blue eyes shift to me for a second before he directs his attention back to Rhys. "We got off around the same time during the shift changeover. Five-thirty, I think." His gaze flits my way again.

I tilt my head, considering him, and pull out my notebook. I write down a random note to give myself something to do while keeping my peripheral aware of Kohen. Most people will avoid eye contact for any length of time. It's common, having an unnerving effect. I'm giving him the opportunity to check me out without catching him to see what he does.

If Rhys notices his conduct, he doesn't let on. "Did you notice anything odd or alarming about Joanna's behavior that day? Did she seem worried or upset?"

Kohen shakes his head. "Not that I could tell."

"When did you leave the Tiki Hive?"

Kohen's gaze lingers on me as he replies. "Not long after Jo did. I have an alibi, if you're going to ask where I was during the time of her death."

Everyone's seen cop shows. Rhys smirks. "And where were you?"

He crosses his arms, defensive. "I was at my mother's house. I do the shopping for her."

"You have a good memory," I say, drawing his attention on me.

He nods slowly. "Yeah, well, I've been in charge of her doctor appointments and medications, and all her shopping for the past three years. I have to have a good memory to keep up with all that, or else bad things happen."

He's looking directly into my eyes as he says this last part.

Rhys bristles at the hostility in his tone and moves a fraction closer to me. I'm not fazed. "What does your mother have?" I ask.

"Late osteosarcoma," he answers.

A chill brushes my skin. "I'm sorry." He nods, but says nothing else on the matter.

Regardless of his place among this case, I do feel regret for him. After Amber was diagnosed with advanced osteosarcoma, she was never the same. I was never the same. Surgery and chemo failed her after a yearlong battle. The cancer had already spread to her lungs by the time it was discovered.

Watching a loved one deteriorate from this debilitating cancer is isolating, painful.

Amber was twelve when she died.

"Do you mind recounting your whereabouts?" Rhys asks, shifting the subject back on track. "Since you have such a great memory, that shouldn't be an issue for us to confirm."

"Sure." Kohen recites his routine for the day of Joanna's murder. Work, pharmacy, and then a trip to the grocery store that put him at his mother's house by approximately six forty-five p.m. Then he spent the evening with her, until about nine-thirty.

"Can anyone corroborate the time you made it back home?" Rhys pushes.

Kohen adjusts his stance. "No. I live alone."

"Why were you let go from the Tiki Hive?" Rhys changes the topic quickly.

"As you can imagine, my mother's failing health takes up a lot of my time. My boss didn't like me coming in late and calling out when I needed to take her to appointments."

Rhys glances at me, a mental tag-in. "There were a few reports from patrons that you made advances on customers during work," I say. "According to your former boss, you were caught giving away free drinks to such customers."

He scoffs. "Those old bats? They're harmless, but they have some wild imaginations." He grins at me, teeth white and straight.

But he knew immediately to whom I was referring. "So their claims are unfounded?" I press.

He takes a step forward, gaining an inch toward me, and Rhys moves in as my shield. Kohen runs a hand through his floppy hair, a smile crooking his lips. "I might have led them on a couple of times," he says. "They were good tippers."

I read between the lines and take a chance. "They solicited you for sex," I say outright.

His smile widens. "Well, really only one of them did." He shrugs. "Times are hard. Got to make the rent. I looked at it more like we were doing each other a favor. I needed money, Vinnie needed someone to sleep with her old ass."

Not a hint of shame in his voice. From what I've gathered so far, Kohen Hayes is a narcissist, with possible borderline sociopathic tendencies. But that doesn't make him a killer. He would need motive to kill Joanna. That motive could be viewed as obscure and loose to most, but for him, it would be seen as deeply personal.

I decide to play to his ego. "Did Joanna ever come on to you? Proposition you with sex for drugs or money?"

He laughs. "What? Uh, no. I was never *propositioned* for sex by her," he mocks.

I raise an eyebrow. "But you knew she had once had a drug addiction?"

He sighs long and hard. "It's Florida. The bowels of hell. Who doesn't?" Before I can ask further, he adds, "Jo was hot, all right? Sure she flirted with me, and I didn't mind one bit. That's how F&B is; everyone fucks with everyone. It eases the tension during a rush." His gaze hardens on me. "Don't read too much into that."

"But maybe Joanna did," I counter. "Maybe she took the flirting as more than just casual workplace banter."

Kohen reaches behind to grab the doorknob, retreating. "I honestly didn't know her that well, so I couldn't tell you."

"You ever show Jo images of your rope fetish?" Rhys does another quick shift. "Shibari, is it? Rope bondage?" We did some fast Googling on the terminology prior.

Kohen sneers. "I think this conversation is over." His gaze slips to me, eyeing the band around my wrist. I tug my shirtsleeve down, and his lips tip into a knowing grin.

Rhys takes out a card and thrusts it toward him. "Thanks for your time. My direct line is on the back. Give me a call if anything else comes to mind."

Hesitantly, Kohen accepts the card. "Yeah." That blue gaze pegs me one last time. "You have a real nice day." I can feel his lingering gaze as I leave.

Once we're in the car, I look at Rhys. "That was abrupt. What is it?"

He cranks the engine and pulls onto the road. "What did you make of him?"

I buckle my seatbelt. "I think he's narcissistic. But the fact that he cares for his mother long term means he may not be psychopathic. Which we know doesn't equate to much in the way of motive to murder, but I couldn't glean any motive from the conversation. You?"

"He said that everyone fucks with everyone in F&B. Torrance claimed Rixon fired Kohen because he was fraternizing with customers, maintaining that the beach bunnies were disturbed by his advances. But according to them, they didn't mind the attention."

I consider this a moment. "I picked up on the same vibe from the women. Claiming that a man—an unnerving man—is hitting on you is a guilt-free way to make yourself feel wanted."

"The beach bunnies didn't come across as modest to me," he says.

I frown his way. "So they liked his attention. I agree that that wouldn't warrant termination from the Tiki Hive, especially if flirtatious banter was acceptable. But Kohen claimed he was let go due to his hindered schedule."

"Then why wouldn't Torrance and Rixon just say that?" Rhys asks.

Good question. "I guess we need to ask them."

A methodical perpetrator would point to a likely suspect without revealing his hand. By directing us toward the beach bunnies, knowing that they may reveal Kohen's preference for bondage, the brothers created a likely suspect.

The fact that Mike didn't mention him during the first investigation only adds to my belief that, if either brother were involved in Joanna's murder, they felt safely removed from the investigation the first time around. Never offer information when not asked. Again, an intelligent person would know this.

At this point, Kohen may still be a suspect, but the brothers have not been removed from the list. If anything, by pointing to Kohen, Torrance made himself even more intrinsic to the case.

As we head toward the coast, I think on that further

and take out my pad to make a note to ask the boyfriend another question. If Joanna was being pursued by either Mike or Torrance, to the point where either one became obsessive enough to fire Kohen because they regarded him as a distraction—or worse, an obstacle—then Joanna might have mentioned any wary feelings about work to Jamison.

Which, also, could put the boyfriend back on the list. Jealousy is one of the deadly murder trifecta.

The case is starting to get murky, but one thing is clear; Kohen is more perceptive than he chooses to appear. Whatever impulse control Kohen lacked in youth, he's acquired now. My impulse was to write him off, but maybe the brothers aren't the only ones using misdirection. We can't clear anyone off the board yet.

The victim's proverbial murder tree is starting to sprout limbs.

BOOK OF DREW

LAKIN: THEN

Being alone with Drew was like being the only woman in the world. When he looked at you—when he looked at *me*—it was as if life up until that point had been an illusion, a deception. Some buried time capsule just waiting for the lid to be ripped off to reveal the real world and all its wonders.

I was awake.

Alive.

Vibrant and beautiful.

He looked right into me; he saw that spark we call a soul. Who I always had been, but was only just discovering with him.

In my youth, I had believed I was content to be second best. That was my place. Amber was the star, and I carved out a quiet corner for myself to exist. And I was happy, or rather, I was content. I didn't know any differently.

Now, I knew someone could love me best. I'd

experienced what it felt like to be desired. We were secluded in our own shiny bubble. Sheltered from that lonely past. And as I stroked his cheek, loving the way his scruff felt against my fingers, the clash of smooth and coarse, I fell harder for him.

I felt brave.

"I love you," I said. There was no shame in admitting this aloud. I trusted Drew with my deepest, darkest fears. My most intimate aspirations. I could trust him with my heart, too.

His eyes flicked over my features before he leaned in and kissed my forehead. "I know you do," he said.

I swelled at his response. I dropped back against the blanket, the beach sand molding to my body. Curves that I had once felt self-conscious about on show in a bikini, but the way Drew's gaze lingered on my flesh made me want to parade up and down the shore.

He leaned over me, blotting out the sun. He was my sun.

"What would you do for that love?" he asked, his finger trailing my thigh.

I shivered at his intimate touch. "Anything," I said. "Everything."

His smile stretched, bright eyes gleamed. Then he moved in closer, his lips brushing my ear. "Anything?"

As he pulled back, those shimmering eyes darkened. Raw, carnal want shone in the depths, and I felt his desire for me. He tipped my chin up, his finger curled beneath. "Would you kill for us?"

I believed I would—I would do whatever it took for us to be together. And in our world, where only we existed, this was acceptable.

I nodded against his hand. "Yes."

"Then it's settled," he said, voice low. "You're deranged." He laughed, and I slapped his arm.

His hand slipped between my thighs then, sending a heated quiver up my legs, a deep ache pinching my sex. I squeezed my thighs against his hand. His mouth came down on mine, tasting me tenderly at first, then savagely, devouring what belonged to him.

His next whispered words tickled my earlobe as he pressed his mouth to the shell of my ear. Heated breath caressed my neck, the spray of ocean misted my legs.

It was perfect.

It was the last happy day I recall spending with Drew. Just a week before Chelsea showed up at his door. Before the attack.

This is the memory I try to keep sacred, untouched. I don't take it out often, because I want to try to preserve the accuracy of it. I want to keep it unblemished. Unchanged.

And yet, somehow I've already managed to lose the words he whispered to me on the beach. No matter how hard I try to remember, to recall what he said...the blackness catches it, burning the memory at the edges like a Polaroid rapidly smoldering, the ashes chasing the flaming embers of my mind.

❧ 18 ❧

PRIMAL INSTINCT

LAKIN: NOW

The last time I was this close to Torrance, he was winking at Cam. Bar towel slung over his shoulder. Cool countenance of a man about to get laid. Though, I remember he was a lot younger somehow. In his interview with Rhys he revealed he's only twenty-eight, yet the years working in the harsh Florida sun has aged him, making him appear older, weathered.

Fine and deep-set lines feather the outer edge of his dark eyes as he regards me with a squinted gaze. "I haven't seen you in so long…" he says, as if we're old pals. "Are you and—" he snaps his fingers "—what's-her-name still friends?"

"Cameron," I supply. I attempt to bend my lips into a smile. Not too bright; that appears odd, off-putting in these circumstances. Just enough of a smile to seem genuine. Interested. Not at all disturbed about this strange encounter. "And yes," I lie. "We still talk."

Torrance nods.

Rhys has coached me when it comes to dealing with suspects. How to be aware of your facial features—what resonates with people versus what alienates them. If only I could apply that to my writing, my editor would probably adore Rhys just as much as the rest of the female population.

I'm trying to focus on Torrance's reaction to me rather than my internal thoughts on him. If he's at all uncomfortable by my presence, he's good at hiding it. He appears as laid back as the night Cam left with him from the Dock House.

"That's good," Torrance says. His gaze distractedly sweeps the Tiki Hive as patrons filter in from the beach. "What can I get you to drink? Water?" He gives me a quick wink.

I squint, trying to decipher if this is some kind of bartender humor. "Nothing. Thanks." I brace my elbows on the bar top. "We won't keep you long."

Before I contact the boyfriend again, Rhys and I are fact checking. Getting both sides of the story from Kohen and the brothers.

"We just have a couple more questions to follow up on," Rhys jumps in. "After speaking with Kohen, we learned that there were some issues taken with his schedule. Particularly his tardiness and missed days due to caring for his ill mother."

Torrance pulls a face, looking befuddled. I wonder what Rhys reads there. "You'd have to ask Mike. It's tricky, you know? You can't just fire people these days. You have to have cause, or else they file unemployment." He shrugs.

I try to imagine Torrance as the author of the notes. What motive could he have? Again, he wasn't a suspect in my case. So if he didn't write the first letter back then, it doesn't make sense that he'd be the one sending them now.

But Mike... Maybe there's something more to him—some sinister element that derives pleasure from the taunt. People get a rush out of true crime and inserting themselves into investigations. The notes could be just that; a false report. Like the prank calls to helplines.

Even as I think this, it feels wrong. The notes feel personal. Aimed at me and not the cases.

Rhys checks the time on his phone. "When does your brother come in today?"

Torrance leans against the bar top. "He has the day off, but he'll be in first thing tomorrow."

Officially done here, Rhys thanks Torrance for his time and we leave the Tiki Hive. "I think that's as much as the brothers are going to offer up," I say. "Time to question the boyfriend again." I'm anxious to get an answer on Joanna's feelings about her job.

"You make the call on that," Rhys says, as we navigate the boardwalk. "Take good notes. I need to check in at Quantico."

"You're flying out?"

His lips thin. "Unfortunately, I have to. Although I really don't like the idea of leaving you here even for a day."

"Are you worried about the note?" I ask.

He drops the shades he bought at the hotel gift shop over his eyes, shielding himself from the sun and me. "Why don't you go with me? Meet the team officially, in person. I can get you a visitor pass."

I've come to learn that with Rhys, it's more about what he leaves unsaid. "Have I ever done that?"

He smiles. The answer: no. He knows I'm not a people person.

"I could visit my parents," I blurt. It just comes out. I try to school my features into a mask that doesn't betray how uncomfortable that statement makes me feel.

I'm sure he can see right through me—but even so, most visits home make people uncomfortable. Me, for a number of reasons. I had always believed that once I left home for college—my brand-new start—I could escape Amber's haunting memory that still hangs over our family like a storm cloud.

My parents visit me in Missouri, occasionally bringing my aunt along. Otherwise, I've barely seen her over the past fifteen years. We effectively evade each other. It's best this way, because the pain I still register in her eyes when she looks at me, as if she's searching for Amber somewhere within and coming up short... Well, some things are better left untouched.

I don't see how Rhys will believe me. Even when he convinced me to return to the Dock House pier to try to unearth my buried memories, I didn't visit my home.

"All right," Rhys concedes. "You want me to drop you off there before I catch a flight?"

We reach the rental car and I wait at the passenger side for him to unlock the door. "It's fine. I can take an Uber. I'll stay at the hotel until then. Work on the case."

That uncertain expression crosses his face again. My mention of the hotel, where the author of the note knows I'm staying. But he nods and gets into the car. "Stay in my room," he says.

I agree without argument. Which should tip him off more than anything that I have no plans to see my parents while he's away.

Three and a half years feels like a lifetime. Theoretically, time is relevant—all based on perception. And since I'm no longer the same person I was back then, I can only imagine how much Cam has changed.

It's not like two friends from the past greeting each other; hugs and smiles and happy tears. We're two strangers.

The social media posts I glance at every once in awhile don't reveal the true person, so I have no idea who she really is now, and I have no idea why I even tracked her down, other than a compulsion to see this to an end.

All I know for sure is that I can't stop looking at her belly as she sits across from me. She's healthy and carrying a healthy baby. And she beams—that pregnancy glow everyone talks about. It's becoming on her.

"Glow," Cam says, dismissively waving her hand through the air. "Please. More like humidity sheen. Sweltering heat glisten." She laughs, but I can hear a thread of unease beneath the throaty cadence.

I shouldn't have come. But as the boyfriend is still out of town on business and was unable to take my call, I told myself I had time—that this needed to happen.

I shouldn't have interrupted her happy life. I'm a painful memory to her—one she's tried hard to forget. Yet this is one thing I can't ignore, that I can't leave unfinished.

I have to know if what I wrote yesterday was an extension of the fiction I've been building all these years, or a recovered memory.

"So did you finish your degree?" she asks, reaching for more small talk.

We're seated on her patio. Large fans are mounted above on the pergola. Sheer white linen is draped between the beams. When I made the call for us to meet, I could barely hear her forced, enthusiastic "yes", my heart thundering in my ears.

I've had her number for over a year.

"I didn't finish college," I admit with a tight smile. "I'm writing now."

"Oh." She nods. "What do you write?"

A dull throb pulses at my temples, like I'm dehydrated. I don't do well with small talk. The meeting with her is already causing too much distress. "Cam, I came here to ask you something."

The atmosphere around us shifts, charged. I can feel her alarm, the way her flip-flop-clad feet point toward the glass-sliding door, already marking her escape. She places her hands on her belly, as if sheltering her baby from my presence, my horrid past, or maybe giving herself some form of comfort.

I wouldn't know.

When she doesn't speak, but doesn't leave either, I push forward. "I need to know about that night, Cam. What actually happened?"

Lowering her gaze, she adjusts the pitcher of tea on the wicker table. "I've already told you everything. There's nothing left to say about it, Cynthia. I'm sorry."

That name feels so foreign to me; my mother and

father the only ones who now address me by my given name.

"I had a flashback yesterday," I say, forcing the subject. "Of us in my hospital room. Of that night…" I trail off. "It's the first time that I've been able to remember a little more from the night of my attack."

She stands. "Is that good?"

I furrow my brow. "It's better than never remembering, isn't it?"

She shakes her head. "I don't know, Cynthia. I don't know. Honestly. With what you endured…" She braces her hands on the table.

"Are you all right?" I go to stand.

"I'm fine. Just Braxton Hicks." As she rights herself, she forces a smile. "I think this is a conversation you should be having with your therapist or whomever. Not me."

I fold my napkin and lay it over the dessert she set out for us. I haven't touched the lemon pie. The whipped cream melted into a puddle on top. "Who was there that night?"

I'm not letting this go. I was *angry* with her. I remember this. Whether the memory was altered in some way, I didn't imagine her behavior in the hospital. She knows more than she told the police—more than she told me.

She releases a lengthy breath. "Just us…and some random people we didn't know. And Torrance, the bartender. Which I've told you and Dutton a million times." She turns to head into her house. "Now, please go."

"I saw Torrance, Cam. He's part of an investigation into a cold case that involves the murder of a woman a year ago. Circumstances much like mine." I pause to let this information sink in. "So is his brother. Did you know he has a brother?"

She looks tired, defeated already. "How the hell would I? I was only with him that one time. Which is a complete blur from being drunk. Oh, and also, from my best friend nearly being murdered. That does tend to make everything else pale. What is it that you want, Cynthia? Why are you here, now? After all this time?"

The burning question.

I'll make him pay…

"Did you see Drew that night?"

Dumbfounded, she sits back down. Pushes her long blond hair behind her ears. "I made him leave," she finally admits.

Nearly four years and so many lies later…

But I realized the only reason why she'd have been so angry with Drew at the hospital was if he had shown up that night. If something else had happened between them.

"Why didn't you say anything?"

She shakes her head absently. "I don't know. The police were already singling him out and—"

"And you *knew* that it couldn't have been him," I say.

Her eyes find mine. Years of buried guilt rises in the sheen. "I told Drew that I'd meet him later," she says. "I didn't sleep with the bartender that night. I left with him, but I didn't follow him to his place."

I nod slowly, the puzzle pieces coming together to finally fill in the gaps. Cam knew that Drew wasn't my attacker because she was with him. "That's why you didn't try to make me leave with you at the Dock House. You said you did, but you left me there. So you could be with

Drew." Her statement to me at the hospital felt false then, I just didn't know why. "Was there anyone *not* sleeping with Drew while we were dating?"

She flinches at my incensed accusation. "It wasn't like that, Cynth."

"Don't call me that. It's not my name." Not anymore.

She swallows hard. "I mean, how could you not know? He was a hot college professor. The epitome of a cliché. I didn't realize how serious you were about him at first… and then, it was only a couple of times after that. I loved you, Cy—" She cuts herself off. "I wasn't with Drew that night. Not like that. I really was angry over the Chelsea situation on your behalf, and I didn't want Drew at the bar hurting you further. So I met him at his house and told him what a douche I thought he was for doing what he did."

Still, the damage is done. She pitied me back then. The introverted, clueless loner who fell for her college professor. I wonder how much of our friendship was based on pity.

"What time was that?" I ask, slipping into my professional persona, suiting up like armor.

"I'm not sure… Maybe around eleven-thirty?"

I make a mental note. "And what time did you see Drew at the Dock House?"

"Cynth—"

"This is not about me," I say, steeling my resolve. "Another woman was killed, possibly more. I need the truth from you now to help her."

She nods. "It must've been about nine or so. It was about an hour before I left with Torrance. I saw Drew lurking around the dock, and I intercepted him before he could approach you and sent him away."

"You told Detective Dutton that you and Torrance left the Dock House at approximately ten p.m." It's comfortable here, in this safe persona. I dig in with my heels. "That's roughly an hour where you don't know where Drew was."

Her eyebrows draw together. "That can't be right. I must have my times wrong. It was so long ago. I swear, Cynthia. I blew Torrance off and headed straight to Drew's. I saw him. I talked to him. There's no way he could've—"

"No, maybe not. But there's a window where I need information and answers." I stand and grab my bag from the back of the chair and shoulder it. "Drew had Chelsea cover for him as his alibi for that night. Why?" I look into her eyes, searching. "Why didn't you both just tell the truth? Why try to hide it after everything?"

"You had been hurt so deeply. Were in so much pain. Physically and emotionally. I just couldn't..." Tears actually brim her eyes. "I couldn't live with myself if I added to that."

I believe her. I'm not sure whether or not I can forgive her, at least not this instant, but I believe her reasoning. Because in the end, it's selfish. Selfish reasons are usually the most honest.

I was pulled from the water, from death, and I assumed for these past few years that the filth and the grime of my soiled life—Drew; Chelsea; everything—was rinsed clean. I was a lotus plucked from the muddy water.

A new life. A fresh start.

Forgotten memories often make it easy to start over.

But Cam has lived with the knowledge of her betrayal all this time.

Maybe that's punishment enough.

"I'm sorry," Cam says again as I leave the patio.

"Me too." I'm sorry for the friendship that I thought we once had, that will now be forever tarnished.

I walk a good distance before I pull up the Uber app and request a ride to the hotel. I need the time to decompress, to think. I was naive in my love for Drew; I know this. After Chelsea... I thought that was where my naivety ended.

Back then, blinded by love, I thought Drew and I were the only two people in the world who were experiencing what we were. I suppose that's what first-time love makes you believe. Reality is a crushing low. How desperate was I to be loved? Genuinely loved? That I trusted him?

But Cam's duplicity stings more than any betrayal on Drew's part.

I snap the rubber band five times, counting aloud to drown out the obsessive thoughts raging inside my head.

Disgusted with myself, I trek across the street toward the sidewalk to wait for my ride, and that's when I get that feeling. The sun is beating down on me, yet the cool prickle touches my skin, leaving cold sweat in its wake across the back of my neck.

I stop at the corner and peer around, heart thudding painfully in my chest. I touch the scars through the flimsy shirt, the one slashed scar that pangs with haunted accuracy any time I sense danger.

All in your mind.

I'm upset. Wounded. Phantom pain can be triggered by extreme emotion, even for those suffering limited emotional range. We bleed just the same.

But the push of fear grows stronger, urging me farther

back on the trail…and I whip my head around to see a figure lurch into a clutch of pine trees.

Animal, my mind pleads.

But it's too large. Too human shaped.

Someone out for a walk.

Only I can feel their gaze on me, watching.

A blue Honda comes around the bend in the road and honks the horn. I jog to the car, fleeing Cam and the past and the truth that I now know.

Someone is following me.

PERFECT STORM

LAKIN: NOW

I'm not a good liar. Let me rephrase: I'm not a good liar to other people. The lies we tell ourselves so that we can cope with our insignificant existence, to make us feel more meaningful in this life, aren't the same as a tailored lie meant to deceive another person.

Rhys is a walking lie detector. Which means the lie I've prepared about visiting my parents sits sour on my tongue. I'm not sure if this is because I know I'll most likely be caught, or whether the thought of lying to Rhys just feels...wrong.

Either way, by the time I hear him enter the keycard into his hotel room door, I've rehearsed the fib too many times in my head for it to come out naturally. So when he asks, "How are your parents?"

I blurt: "I went to see Cameron."

It's midnight and he doesn't look jetlagged in the least.

His slate-gray eyes are clear and alert, and they're assessing me coolly, calmly.

He sets his duffle bag down in the corner, then peels off his suit jacket. "Did she know Mike Rixon?"

The breath I've been holding eases out. Rhys doesn't do confrontation. If he had been upset, felt deceived, he'd have simply left the room without a word. I'd rather he admonish me for being reckless than suffer his stone-cold silent treatment. It's hard to bring him back from that.

I tug my long T-shirt down my thighs and cross my ankles on the bed. "She seemed like she had no idea that Torrance had a brother."

"Did you show her a picture of him? See if she recognized Rixon from the Dock House?" Black tie hung loose around his neck, he removes his shoulder harness and takes a seat across from me on the bed.

"No. I didn't..." I should have, and I probably would've thought to do so had I not been so focused on Drew. "And the element of surprise is gone now. Going back to ask probably won't render any new information on that front. Especially since we didn't part on the best of terms."

The stern contort of his expression relaxes at this. "I take it she wasn't exactly happy to dredge up the past."

I glance at the floor. "She lied to me," I say. "I don't know why I didn't realize it before. I can't blame faulty memory there; I knew something was off. I just didn't know what or didn't *want* to know. Maybe." When I look at him, the commiseration I glean in his eyes is a comfort. "She'd been sleeping with Drew." I barrel ahead before he can start an interrogation. I fill him in on everything Cam revealed. "She claims she wasn't with him in that capacity the night of the attack, but that she was with him at his house. That he couldn't have possibly went back to the Dock House."

Rhys takes it all in, then says, "Not unless he never left."

Alarm skitters through me at that realization. "The drive from the bar to Drew's house then is over an hour."

"It would be tight, but we don't actually know the time of your attack. It could've been an hour after Cam left, or it could've been five minutes. Which would make it possible."

And Drew allowing Cam to come over gives him a conspirator—two alibis in case one falls through. "Drew told her not to tell the police the truth, probably claiming that it would hurt me further and damage our friendship. He knew he'd be a suspect, and sleeping with my best friend and roommate would make him look even worse to the case detectives."

Rhys nods knowingly. "We profiled your attacker as intelligent and cautious. Abbot always appeared that way to me."

Which means if Drew was behind my attempted murder, he put thought into it. Premeditated. Not a crime of chance.

I stand, feeling sick. Start to pace. "I never thought, not once, not really, that Drew could be behind it...that he could be capable..."

Even when Cam revealed he was at the bar, it just didn't compute. What reason did he have to want to harm me—to want me *dead*? I wasn't the one pregnant. I wasn't a threat to his freedom or his career. "It makes no sense," I whisper to myself.

Lost in thought, I don't realize Rhys is standing behind me until I feel the charge of his skin near mine. He touches my arm, and I flinch.

"It's all right," he says, but he removes his hand as I turn to face him.

I cross my arms, acutely aware of the thin material of my shirt, the only thing I'm wearing other than boy shorts, the flimsiest of barriers between us. "Do you think he could've really done this to me?"

Rhys knows people. He reads suspects and motives. His opinion is the only one that matters.

He removes his necktie, wraps it around his hand as he considers this. He exhales heavily, then: "I don't know."

His admission shocks me. I shake my head, unable to accept that Rhys doesn't at least have a theory. "You interviewed him. You've had to consider the prospect before now. That Dutton missed something, or just couldn't put it together—"

"And I did. I have," he cuts in, his voice low, worn. "What is Abbot's motive, Hale?"

Right. Motive. A weight sits heavily on my shoulders.

"Think," Rhys urges. "After seeing Cam, does anything come back to you? Anything at all?"

I look away as the same unsettling anxiety creeps over me—the one I experienced when Rhys and I returned to the Dock House. Back then, he implored me to remember, *to think*... As if all I had to do was tap into those memories and the answers would tumble free.

"It's so frustrating," I say, shaking my head. "Being back here."

His frown deepens. "I know." A short beat. "We looked at Drew hard when we first reopened your case, but just like now, even after this new information, we're unclear on motive."

I deflate. I'm not sure if Drew's lack of motive is a comfort, but it's damn infuriating.

"What I do know," he says, moving a fraction closer, "is that people respond to threats oddly. I've worked on cases where a perpetrator's motive made no logical sense to me, but it's not about me. It's not even about you. If Abbot is good for this, then he had his reason. Whether or not you'll ever be able to understand it…well, that might be the hardest part to live with."

I stare into his eyes. "Even harder than not knowing?"

He's so close now, I can smell his aquatic cologne. His body heat touches my skin, making me yearn to press against him and absorb his warmth.

The thought sends a jolt of awareness through me.

"You've worked cold cases," he says, drawing me out of my thoughts. "You know there's never any satisfaction at the end of the tunnel. There's truth, there's a form of closure, of justice. But there's no gratification."

He's right, of course. How many times have I longed to know what the families felt when I'm writing their story, only to sit in front of my laptop, blank. Stalled. Unable to find the words.

I rub my arms, chasing away the sudden chill of the A/C unit. "Okay," I say, accepting. "Then we just follow the lead."

"To wherever it takes us."

My gaze snaps to his. *Us.*

"I think I was being followed." It just comes out. The need to divulge the utter truth to Rhys may be lingering guilt from my former mistruth, or something else—

something I see in his eyes; that yearning my brain says to ignore, to avoid.

His expression darkens. "Where?"

"After I left Cam's. Not far from her house. I thought I saw a man." I shrug. "Maybe it was nothing." But the note resurfaces fresh in my mind. Someone wants me off the case.

"Did you see what he looked like?" Rhys forces the subject.

"Tall. Could've even been a woman. They dipped into the tree line as soon as I spotted them." It sounds stupid to hear myself say it aloud.

Rhys is still holding my arms; his grasp tightens. "You can't go off solo," he says. "Until we prove otherwise, we have to take this seriously. Someone sent that note. That person doesn't want you working the Delany case, or they fear…" He trails off.

"That I'll make the connection to my own case?"

I can see it in the hard press of his lips, the painful realization that he's refusing to admit. My stalker is connected to my past. This person could be the key, if he doesn't end my pursuit first.

If he doesn't kill me.

What's he waiting for?

"I don't want to talk about this now," I say, trying to step out of his hold.

His dark brows draw together. "There's more," Rhys says, reading me clearly. "What else, Hale?"

I try to turn away, but he holds on. Strong fingers embed my flesh. This time, he's not letting go. "Tell me."

Even as I try to push it away, the image of Cam on her patio flares vividly in my mind. "Cam. She's pregnant."

God, I'm pathetic. I came here to solve Joanna's case, to bring a murderer to justice. Not wallow in self-pity.

I should've never come back.

I note the slackening of Rhys's hands. He softens at my admission. Then his palms graze my arms, a comforting caress that should feel foreign coming from him, but it's the most natural touch. Like he touches me in this way all the time.

Everything that could be said is relayed through that touch. How sorry he is that this was taken—*stolen*—from me. That I'll never experience this miracle for myself. That I'll never be a mother.

An ache pushes against the back of my eyes, the threat of tears, but I sniff them back. I won't succumb to grief.

I'm alive.

Joanna's not.

Rhys attempts to say something, but I stop him. Fearful of what my reaction might be if he opens up to me right now.

"It's not...I'm fine." I force a tense smile. "Besides, that's the furthest thing I should be thinking about."

His hands move to my shoulders. He's somehow even closer, his towering height making me feel sheltered, protected. A strange mix of security and tantalizing heat charges the air between us. It's torturous, this confusing combination that I've never felt near Rhys before—only it feels as if it's not unfamiliar; like past and present colliding; the way it's always been.

He cups my face. His thumb strokes my jawline, my skin heating at his tender touch. The way he's looking at me... He kissed me once—just the one time. By the lake, when he pressed his lips gently to my forehead. It was done in a way a brother or a friend might kiss you; consolingly.

But intent is everything, and I do not see the intent to console me in his burning gaze now. There's a ravenous hunger blazing in the depths of his irises. I'm torn over whether I meet him there—whether I should lean in or pull away.

"Lakin...I have to tell you..." His voice is thick, a guttural whisper that reverberates the warring emotions within me. I'm Hale to Rhys. His partner. Who is Lakin the woman to him?

His mouth nears mine, so close I can feel the warmth of his uneven breaths, when the ringing starts.

It's the hotel room phone.

I awaken and take a step back. His hands fall away, and I already miss the feel of them. His gaze holds mine one second too long, a question there. It says if he walks away right now, we may never get this moment back. If he walks away...we'll never admit to it.

I hesitate a fraction of a second...

Before I can voice anything, he turns to answer the phone.

I listen to him have a brief conversation with the hotel management, my emotions a swirling vortex, and then he hangs up the receiver.

"What is it?" My heart still thuds heavily in my chest.

Rhys drives a hand through his hair. "The locals know we're working the Delany case. One of the case detectives left a message for us at the desk."

It usually doesn't take long for law enforcement to get wind of the FBI reopening a cold case. Some take offense to us encroaching on their turf, thinking we're out to make them look bad, like they didn't do their job, if we solve the case where they couldn't.

"Are you going down there?" I hate the tremble of my voice, the ragged want that resonates.

Rhys releases a breath, tucks his hands in his pockets. "Not tonight." His gaze lifts to meet mine.

There's still that question hovering between us, as if I can reach out and grasp it. Bring the moment back from just two minutes ago. It's my choice. As he waits me out, I know it's all mine.

I'm a coward.

I glance around the room, then head toward my side of the bed. "I guess dealing with the locals can wait until morning." I drag back the covers and crawl underneath, shivering at the cool caress of the sheets. So acutely different than his heated touch.

This can't happen.

I know once the sun comes up, I'll feel differently. He'll feel differently. It's the late hour. It's my vulnerability. His protective nature. We've created a perfect storm, and the morning light will disperse the vapors.

I rest my head against the pillow and watch as Rhys readies himself for bed. He turns off the lamp. "Night, Hale."

20

NEXUS

LAKIN: NOW

There are three primary motives for murder: sex, money, and revenge.

Since that night, I've wondered what my attacker's motive was. I wasn't rich. I wasn't raped. And at the time, what could I have done in my short twenty-three years to warrant that level of sadistic revenge?

I think about the murder board back at my Missouri home. Countless hours invested in the rebuilding of my case. Every player has at least one black line drawn in connection to the event. But it's conjecture. Circumstantial. What's important and relevant to me is not so much to the detectives.

Rhys has never seen my murder board.

When there appears to be no obvious motive, there's the question of whether or not the murder could be serial in nature. A serial killer typically has no connection to his victims. Sometimes there's a victimology, his victim selection process, where the offender is meticulous, systematic, and other times a victim is chosen at random. Possibly out of convenience.

This is the reason law enforcement becomes confounded when working serial killer cases. They depend on the victim's link to the killer to find him, and when there is no link...

Well, I believe there is always a link. No matter how tenuous. The nexus may just be too minute for caseworkers to consider it significant.

A look. Bat of the lashes. A smile.

One single moment caught, suspended in time. And you're in his web.

I'm not blaming the victim; the connection is misconstrued by the perpetrator. Serial killers rationalize, quite elaborately, their justifications. The actions taken are always in the killer's control.

So how does a surviving victim take back that control?

I'm still searching for the answer.

Cam's past betrayal has possibly implicated Drew. At least opened the door to question him further. That may lead to more information. I should feel relieved—one step closer.

I believed once that control was restored when the killer was caught.

Rhys's declaration is a sobering truth. The never-ending quest for gratification is a dark, bottomless pit. Even darker than my underwater tomb.

Before I move forward, I have to decide if catching my attacker will restore the balance of control. Or send me spiraling down.

Coffee nestled in my lap, we pull up to the Brevard

County Medical Examiner's Office. The parking lot is near empty, and Rhys snags a spot in front of the brick building. We open the car doors to the humid morning air.

I take one last sip of coffee and then set it on the floorboard.

Even now, I need to know. Despite the warning, *in spite* of my own detriment, I'm more determined than ever to find my killer.

Before we left the hotel, Rhys picked up the message from Detective Vale. The detective is aware that we're working the Delany case and wants us to come to the precinct. We'd eventually work our way to the detectives, to get their insight, but we try to save that interview for last. Not wanting to taint our own investigation at the start.

With the morning came a fresh perspective, last night safely and securely locked in its own secret compartment as part of the past. Rhys and I decided we'd postpone the interrogation (as nearly every meeting with major crimes and detectives results in them questioning *us*), and instead get the pertinent information on Joanna's murder right from the source. That way we can start building the case backward.

Sounds confusing. Well, it is. Mystery writers often use this tactic to create a who-done-it storyline. Solve the crime first, then work backward planting clues for the reader.

I'm picturing Rhys and I as very clueless readers today. We need the end—Joanna's end—so we can work backward toward her attack.

Rhys rings the doorbell, then inserts his hands in his pockets. "I have to send in a formal update to Quantico today," he says. "At some point."

"But you just got back from checking in," I say. "Do we have anything to file yet?"

He blows out a terse breath. "No. But my superiors don't care about individual cases. They just want to see progress from the team as a whole."

My eyebrows draw together. I don't envy Rhys this part of the job. He gets the bureaucratic bullshit, while I get to weave stories in my comfy glider.

"Shouldn't take long to work up a report that shows the team's involvement," he says, rocking on his heels and tapping the doorbell once more. "You want to call home? Check in on your cat and neighbor?"

A guilty twinge pangs my chest. I've been so consumed by the case, by my past, that I haven't thought to do so on my own. And honestly, ever since I revealed Cam's confession to Rhys last night, I've been agitated, impatient for us to question Drew. I've snapped the rubber band six times already this morning.

"Yes. I will," I say.

"You could still fly back for a day," he says, not meeting my eyes. "Check in on them properly while I handle the paperwork."

"I don't know. Seems like unnecessary mileage if I'm just turning around to come right back…" As I say this, I realize I might not be returning—that maybe this is the point.

Rhys never voiced his disapproval of my meeting with Cam, but I know it's still simmering between us. A cold splash of betrayal slaps me. I trust Rhys more than anyone; he'd never deliberately deceive me. Is this about me being followed?

Before I'm able to voice my concern, the glass door

clicks open. Dr. Keller, the district medical examiner, is dressed in green scrubs. I recognize him from his picture on the website.

"Can I help you?" Dr. Keller greets us.

Rhys flashes his FBI shield. "Dr. Keller, I'm Special Agent Rhys Nolan, and this is my partner, Lakin Hale. I'm hoping you have time this morning to answer a few questions we have on a past case."

I smile to myself. Rhys may dismiss psychology, but he often uses it to his advantage. He never gives people the opportunity to *not* answer his questions. He just gives them the option to do it now, or later.

In his late-forties, with patches of gray-and-black hair peeking from beneath his cap, the district pathologist frowns. "I'm sorry, but could this be done another day? I'm in the middle of an autopsy."

Rhys tucks his badge into the inseam of his suit jacket. "We're only in town for a few days, and we'd really like to get a firsthand account from the expert on Joanna Delany's case."

Dr. Keller tilts his head. The victim's name seems to pique his interest. "All right, come on back. You'll need to wash up and don scrubs."

Rhys and I exchange a curious glance before we enter the building. An interview doesn't require us to dress for an examination.

"Maybe he's in a rush and plans to talk to us while working," I say.

"Maybe," Rhys agrees, but he's distracted. I can sense he's already two mental steps ahead.

Dr. Keller directs us toward a bank of sinks. "Fresh

scrubs are hanging up over there." He points to the partition.

"What are you thinking?" I ask as we wash our hands. Sometimes I wish I could get an inside look into his thoughts.

"Not sure yet." Rhys shakes off the water, then grabs one of the green robes.

Once we're fully covered, Dr. Keller walks us behind the partition. "It's interesting you should bring up the Delany case," the pathologist says. "A female victim was discovered just yesterday. I recognized the lacerations right away during my initial exam at the scene. I pulled the Delany file this morning to compare."

The body on the morgue table is pale, the Y incision already cut into the victim's sternum. I cover my mouth and quickly look away, catching my breath.

"Is she all right?" the doctor asks.

"She's fine," Rhys answers for me. "This just wasn't on the agenda."

"Oh," Dr. Keller remarks. "Here. Let me get you some Vics. The victim hasn't been dead long, so I didn't think the smell was too bad. Of course, I really don't notice it anymore."

He attempts a weak smile, and I nod. "Just a bit shocking…when you're not expecting it."

"Even without the smell, the mint in the rub helps quell the nausea from the sight." He hands me the Vic's Vapor Rub. "A kind of numbing, cure-all for the senses."

"Thank you." I dab a fingertip into the ointment and smudge it beneath my nose. "Just needed to get my bearings."

Truthfully, this is the first dead murder victim I've seen in person. Working cold cases, you get used to the pictures. After staring at mutilated corpses for a few years, I believed I built up a tolerance, a defense. But with images you're removed, distanced. It's not the same as real life.

Nothing prepares you for this.

Then the doctor pulls back the sheet covering the victim's face.

And the woman on the gurney is no longer just a body.

The floor shifts, and I vertically right myself to keep balance. *Oh, God. No.*

I press my hand to the partition, thinking that will somehow stop the spinning motion. "Cam…"

Dr. Keller approaches me cautiously. "You know the victim?"

"Knew—" I *knew* her.

"Then, I'm sorry, but you can't be here."

I feel Rhys's hand on my arm, steadying me. "We're not working this case. We're on the Delany cold case with the cold case division."

"I'm sorry for your loss," Dr. Keller says.

"Thank you," I manage, but it feels wrong to accept his condolences. I hadn't been Cam's friend for a long time. Although, when you stretch the seams of time out, what length is considered a long enough time not to be someone's friend?

I met Cameron freshman year. We were the same age. Both excited and scared and curious. Three years as college roommates, as best friends, then the world changed, and it's been too many years since we've spoken.

Until yesterday.

What does that equate to?

Rhys and Dr. Keller are talking, muffled voices float to my ears. Then I catch one word more clearly than the others—one word that freezes my blood.

Baby.

Cam was pregnant.

Through my blurred vision, I study her shape. The flatness of her stomach. The missing swell of her belly that I was so envious over the day before.

"What happened?" I hear myself ask.

The ME looks to Rhys, silently conspiring what's proper to reveal to me.

"I can handle it," I say, forcing my voice steady.

Rhys takes my arm in a calm hold and faces me. I see it in his eyes then: the warning.

Implication.

He doesn't express his fear aloud. He doesn't have to. I was one of the last people to see Cam alive. I might've been *the* last person. Considering the timing, the call from Detective Vale might've been a ruse. Bring me in to discuss the cold case and corner me in an interrogation room.

My hands tingle. I can feel the blood draining from my extremities, adrenaline taking hold. My pulse quickens.

She's dead because of me.

"The baby survived," Dr. Keller says. "It's extremely rare. A baby only survives inside the womb for mere minutes after the mother's death."

Relief floods me, and I nearly crumple to the floor. It only lasts a moment, though. Had I never gone to visit Cam, chances are, she'd still be alive. I know it in my bones that I was followed yesterday.

"How was that possible?" Rhys asks.

"I'm not working that side of it," Dr. Keller says, "but I believe the police received a call-in. Paramedics arrived in time."

In time to save the baby. But not Cam.

Who called it in?

"The victim's femoral artery was severed," Dr. Keller continues, giving his attention to the body. "That was the cause of death. She was stabbed eight times, but every laceration"—he points to the deep wounds on her chest—"was survivable on its own. I want to believe the perpetrator purposely missed exposing the fetus to any harm."

The fetus. The way he says it...so technical...I swallow hard. I do the same; detach myself from the crime. In my case, I have to. I can't identify with the victim. It's too dangerous. Rhys has drilled this into me.

But this is Cam.

As I look at her pale body, lifeless, all the vibrant colors that made her alive drained from her flesh, I can't remove myself. The terrible irony that Cam's end was met with the fate that should've been mine...

What were my last words to her?

I look away. Sickness roils my stomach. "Where is the wound located that caused her death?" Cam's baby was spared. I can see clearly enough to note the killer didn't inflict the same wound to her torso that I suffered. That would've injured the baby.

"Hale, we should leave." Rhys's tone conveys his increasing fear. The more I know, the longer I'm here, the worse it becomes for me.

Dr. Keller moves swiftly to uncover the legs. "Here."

He mimics the direction that the weapon took across her thigh. "Right below her pelvis region. Deep enough to sever the femoral artery, but not deep enough to hit the femur."

"Was it intentional?" Rhys asks.

The ME frowns. "I would have to say yes. Whoever the perpetrator was, he knew enough. This incision was done with a steady hand. No hesitation marks. The location was selectively chosen, also."

"How so?" Rhys can't help it; the agent in him has to have answers.

"The victim bled out quickly, but not so quickly to endanger the fetus. I can't say with one hundred percent conviction that was the intent, but I've been doing this a long time." He wipes his goggles clean. "I trust my instincts."

A rare statement for a man in the medical field. I glance at Rhys. He harbors respect for those who trust their instincts. It's one of the main differences between us.

"Thank you for your honesty," I say to Dr. Keller. He nods his sympathies as I turn to go.

I'm steps away from escaping, but the realization that this is the last time I will see Cam halts my retreat. With a deep, chemical-laced breath, I pull the surgical gown tight around my middle and walk toward the table.

Rhys catches my wrist, and a flash of last night assaults my senses. The imploring I saw in his eyes, the need for me to close the distance between us. His hold on me now pleads for me to stop. Not to torture myself. Don't let this be my last memory of Cam.

"I'm all right." I pull away and move closer to the

table. "I'm sorry," I whisper to her, only loud enough for me to hear.

I can't bring myself to promise Cam what I vow to the others—the victims I try to avenge by catching their killers. How can I make that oath to her? How can I, when her murder is so entwined with mine?

I wait on the other side of the partition as Rhys conducts the interview we primarily came here to obtain. Joanna has—momentarily—taken a backseat as my thoughts drift to the moments I shared with Cam.

Paradoxically, I don't consider myself sentimental, but death has a way of making us just that. We mourn for what can never be again, even when it wasn't a part of our current story.

It's the fear of the absolute end. Finality.

It reminds us with a cold, sobering awareness that we're mortal.

I listen as Rhys goes through the checklist with the pathologist. DNA profile on the vic. What trace was found on the body, if any. Cam's contusions are congruent with the bruises found on Joanna.

Dr. Keller needs to make the proper comparisons, but he believes the lacerations—the deep cut Cam sustained to her thigh; the cut across Joanna's ribs—will be a close match. And if so, he can prove the same weapon was used in both crimes.

I step around the partition.

"Can you use pictures to make a comparison?" I ask.

Dr. Keller's features pull tight. "I can, of course."

My hands grip the hem of my shirt.

"Lakin…" The dark note in Rhys's tone makes me pause. His voice breaks at the end of my name. I wonder if it's because he rarely uses it, or if there's a painful emotion he's trying to conceal.

Our eyes meet. "It could help connect the cases," I say. "We have to know."

I have to know.

He reads that certainty in my eyes; he knows that whatever happens now, I'm bound to uncover the truth.

Rhys lowers his gaze as I lift my shirt above my bra, exposing the ugly, diagonal slash across my chest.

Momentarily stunned, Dr. Keller stares at the scar, speechless. Then he pulls himself out of his daze and grabs his camera from the tray. He takes a few pictures, very professional. Then: "When did this happen?"

"Almost four years ago," I answer. "Will that hinder the comparison? Because it's healed—"

"It shouldn't. I can make the needed adjustments." He makes a note on a pad. "Is there a case file?" His deep-set eyes catch mine. "I need the details to make an accurate comparison. Hospital records will work."

I nod knowingly as I lower my shirt. "Everything about the attack was documented." I leave out that I have no actual memory of it. He'll find out the details soon enough.

Before we leave, Rhys shakes Dr. Keller's hand and thanks him, then we exit the morgue. The coffee I set on the floorboard is still warm. Time passes in its own measure. A torturous lifetime inside the morgue; fifteen minutes to the outside world.

I toss the cup away.

As Rhys and I leave in silence, that one niggling question of motive batters my brain. Why Cam? Why Joanna?

Why me?

I'm the nexus, that much is clear now. The black lines all stem from me to connect the other murders, like the lotus stalks descending down into that dark, underwater world of the unknown.

A look. Bat of the lashes. A smile.

What monster did I lure into our lives?

21

BOOK OF DREAMS

LAKIN: THEN

Aloneness.

Three synonyms: Isolation. Seclusion. Solitude.

Aloneness is not a bad state. For the most part, back then, I was used to being alone. So I didn't mind, not really. There's a difference between being alone and being lonely.

There was a before and after to my life.

Before Amber died of osteosarcoma, and after.

Then there was Andrew Abbot.

It makes me sound insanely vapid. As if I was one of those clingy, insecure college girls who changed personalities for their boyfriends. But for me, having been so utterly isolated up until the moment he drew me out of my shell, it was a rebirth. An awakening.

I was a woman. A real woman. And I was in love.

The world was hued in pink promise and rosy adoration.

Hence, I was naively blind to who Drew actually was. After the fallout, I would learn the true definition of loneliness. Two weeks before the attack, symptoms of what was to come were already appearing in a dream. A recurring nightmare spawned out of fear of losing Drew.

Fear can wreck a mind.

The dream started in the middle, like all dreams do. No beginning.

For some reason, as I write this scene, Drew's lecture on memories is forefront. I'm not sure if this chapter will make it past the editing phase. I'm already tempted to delete the words. As if putting them in print will alter the past.

How do I want to remember the dream?

Was it bright and sunny?

Was it overcast and gloomy?

Maybe it was just after sunset, the evening air thick with the scent of marsh, the crickets chirring loudly in my ears. My skin was tacky with the humidity. My T-shirt clung my back as I crossed onto the wooden planks.

A *bang* crashed through the brush like the crack of a bat against a tree.

I thought of that old metaphor: If a tree falls in the forest and no one is around to hear, does it make a sound?

There was a shadowy presence, a foreboding, engulfing me. I could sense it in the misty air. It pressed heavily from all around. I had to keep moving. I didn't run, but I knew I was being chased.

I'm suddenly in the center of a pier. It stretched out far over a marshy lake. Graffiti decorated the dock in bright, neon spray-paint ahead of me. As I walked closer, I realized it wasn't graffiti.

Fresh slashes of red streaked the darkened, rotted wood.

Blood.

Then I sensed the person nearing. They had found me…

According to dream interpretation, there's a significance to a faceless or unseen entity in a dream. It can signify that the dreamer is searching for their own identity.

Despite my regard for psychoanalysis, I'm not entirely certain I believe this theory (sorry, Freud), or if dream interpretation can quantify on the same level as psychology in general. But during that point in my life, I wasn't knowledgeable on the subject. All I knew was that, amid the dream, the presence terrified me.

This entity was an ominous threat. A tailored demon to haunt my waking world as well as my dreams. Like a dark, sordid truth we keep buried in our psyche, this malevolence wanted to be realized. It wanted to be known, to be made flesh.

Look… The disembodied voice intoned.

The daylight was gone; the night dense with absolute blackness. The sounds of insects so loud I covered my ears. I looked down into the murky water surrounding the pier.

The white water lilies stood stock-still in the water. No breeze to disturb their petals.

Every lotus pond and lake I've ever seen has always been monochromatic. Either white, or yellow, or pink. But never a mix of colors. So the one lone yellow lotus I glimpsed floating amid the others…

A chill slithered down my back at the sight. It was a

lock of blond hair draped over the flower. The same color of her hair.

Chelsea.

I reached down to clear the flowers aside, and a face appeared. Her pale skin looked porcelain against the murky water. Her eyes were open and opaque, colorless, staring at the night sky. Her light-blue shirt was torn at the neckline, revealing jagged scrapes and cuts along her chest and neck. A dark-red wound slashed her breast.

Then the sun peeked. The crisp sunlight played over the white petals, casting splinters of gold around her dead body like a halo. Only, as I continued to stare—just as quickly as a sequence changes within a dream—it was no longer Chelsea in the water, buried in a floating halo of lotuses.

It was a trick of the light, a trick of my mind. After a few months, I even started to believe I might have embellished this part; my creative mind layering details around the memory of the dream.

I was looking at my own face.

Dread encapsulated me, stealing my breath. My chest caved. And then I felt every wound slash my body at once. The pain overwhelmed my senses. Everywhere I touched…my hands were covered in red. My clothes soaked with blood and grimy lake water.

I fought my legs to stand, then looked down the dock, the way I'd come. I was unnervingly calm.

I saw her nearing then. Her golden tan, blond hair white as angel's breath. Her belly was swollen. A slight baby bump denoting her pregnancy.

I'm pregnant.

Chelsea terrified me. My wounds…my imminent

death... I accepted. But the beautiful, confident girl holding her belly protectively ripped through my mind like a twister, decimating and cruel.

I'd never felt so alone like I did when I came out of the dream. Each and every time. Over the course of those two weeks leading up to spring break, I was scared to sleep. Scared to lose Drew. Scared of being alone.

Up until Chelsea showed up at Drew's doorstep, I didn't truly believe in premonitions. Technically, I still don't. I understand the laws of physics and the mind too well. I know that our memories are unreliable—that trauma can alter the way we recall those memories. I know that fear and loss and despondency can manufacture lucid dreams that feel like premonitions in themselves but...

Then there is the man.

Hallucinations are firing neurons—I know this, too. But is it all just a misfiring network in the brain? Or is there some higher level of consciousness that our minds are able to tap into?

There is no answer; only the question.

I saw myself die. It's an uncommon phenomenon to witness oneself die without waking up before that moment of demise. I have no real memory of my death, and yet I witnessed my life end in the dream.

It's a bone-hollowing loneliness, the cold void of fading away.

If a girl dies in a lake and no one is around to see, is she truly dead?

22

PRIME SUSPECT

LAKIN: NOW

"Are you sure you want to do this?"

I stare through the sedan's windshield at the packed parking lot. We're parked at the emergency wing of the hospital where Cam's baby was admitted.

Rhys's hands are gripped to the wheel, the engine idling, as if he's waiting for me to change my mind.

"I need to do this." I clasp the door handle.

"I'll go with you." Rhys finally shuts the car off and opens his door.

"Wait," I say, but I'm not sure what comes next.

Technically, we should be at the West Melbourne precinct. To feel them out, Rhys placed a call and spoke with Detective Right, inquiring about the cold case. As I suspected, the locals want to question me in relation to Cam, not the cold case. By coming here, one could claim we're evading the police. Well, *I'm* evading.

I was the one who went to see Cam yesterday. I'm the

one who has been requested to make a statement to the case detective.

And logically, I won't be permitted access to Cam's baby, anyway. It was born eight weeks premature—a C-section performed on a dead mother. It's like a gruesome headline ripped from the tabloids.

But I owe it to Cam to check on her baby, to make sure she or he is healthy. I never even asked her about the sex. Honestly, it's more peace of mind for myself; a selfish need to know that my visit with Cam, at least, didn't take the life of an unborn child.

I need to see with my own eyes that it's alive.

I need to know if it's a girl or a boy—I need to know the name.

Most days, I like to pretend I'm a vigilante writer hunting killers to avenge the dead, but inherently, I'm a selfish person. Solving cold cases brings a measure of sanity to my otherwise disturbed and unruly world. It gives me a sense of control.

I'm in control of nothing.

"Okay. I'm ready." I open the car door and step into the blistering heat. It takes my breath away.

I drop my shades over my eyes and hike my bag onto my shoulder. Rhys trails behind as I walk through the double-doors of the ER. The *whoosh* of cool air blasts my face, and I shiver.

That's another thing about Florida. Residents keep the A/C at an equally opposite degree to the temperature outside. It's always freezing inside any indoor establishment.

As we approach reception, I push my shades up and note two uniforms positioned at the ER wing entrance.

Rhys steps in front of me before I reach the desk. "This is a bad idea, Hale." He nods to the uniforms. "You're not going to get any information on Cam's baby. The only thing you're going to do is make the detectives more curious about you."

"I know but—" I stop short, his concerned expression shutting me down. There's a note of apprehension in his voice. "You're worried."

"I am."

But it's more. Rhys has always been direct. He doesn't try to placate me. So his avoidance to be candid in this moment is distressing.

"Are you worried because you fear I had something to do with her death?"

His gaze hardens. He takes my wrist and leads me toward a bank of seats, where it's more private. "Did you really just ask me that?"

A pang of guilt stabs my chest. I cross my arms. "I did," I say. "I don't know what any of it means. But I do know the only connection is *me*. You have to see that."

A muscle jumps along his jaw, gaze trained hard on me. "Joanna Delany isn't connected."

"At a glance, it appears that way. But what if we're wrong? We have to keep looking, even if that means implicating me."

He doesn't like this answer, but it's what we do.

"Rhys, Cam was murdered because of me. Because I went to see her. Because—" I lower my voice "—whoever is behind the notes doesn't want me dredging up the past. Cam must've known…"

What?

She admitted that she went to Drew that night. Which

means, for some reason, Torrance the bartender lied to the police about being intimate with her. Because of his ego? Because she asked him to? That doesn't make sense; she'd only just met him. He had no reason to cover for her.

Everyone lies. This is the only truth that I know for sure. Everyone lies, and they do so, typically, for their own selfish purpose.

What else did Cam know? Who else could she implicate? And what does any of it have to do with Joanna Delany?

"Notes?"

Rhys cuts into my thoughts, and I blink up at him. "What?"

"You said 'notes'. What other note?"

Damn. I rub my forehead, stalling. I never told him about the anonymous letter I received before I left Silver Lake. When we reopened my case, I didn't think it was relevant—but it was relevant when another letter showed up in the hotel room.

"I should've told you," I say.

His expression morphs from confusion to anger. I've only seen him angry—truly angry—once before, when the belligerently drunk brother of a victim tried to impede our investigation. The brother had accepted money from a tabloid press, making false statements against his deceased sister to drum up more interest in her murder. Rhys shoved him up against a wall, his fist nearly making contact with his face.

We were both rightfully disgusted.

But Rhys was furious.

Having his fury directed on me feels like a knife to the

gut. A comparison I can accurately make. "Let's go," he says, voice level.

"We can't leave…"

"We are leaving. You're going to tell me everything about the notes before you make a statement."

I allow Rhys to guide me toward the exit.

"Lakin Hale?"

On reflex, I start to turn, but Rhys intercepts me and keeps us on course. "Keep walking."

"Ms. Hale? Wait—"

We're stopped right before the double-doors. A detective catches up with us and blocks our path. I know who he is by the cheap blazer and cop belt before he flashes his badge.

"Detective Vale with the WMPD," he says. "I believe you spoke with my partner not long ago. Funny. I didn't expect to see you so soon, or here."

Rhys straightens his back. "How can we help you, detective?"

The detective's thick face blanches, flustered from either the heat or Rhys's dismissive tone. He looks to me instead of replying to Rhys. "You wouldn't be trying to avoid me, would you, Ms. Hale?"

I rein in my nerves. "If I were, would I be here?" I glance around the waiting room, eying the uniforms. "I'm happy to speak with you, but I don't think this is an appropriate place. Can I schedule a time to meet with you at the precinct?"

"Schedule?" He chuckles. "Sorry, ma'am. I don't work on schedules. As I'm sure you're well aware, time is of the essence. First hours of a murder investigation are crucial." He looks down at me and narrows his gaze.

Apparently, he expects me to answer his rhetorical question.

I raise my eyebrows. "Yes, I know this."

He stuffs his large hands into his pockets. "I do have the privacy of the ER, though. We can speak right through there." He cocks his head toward the emergency wing.

"I'm sorry. I think that's far less appropriate." I attempt to go around him, but he blocks my exit.

"I can get you access to see the baby," he says, and my heart knocks. "That's why you're here, right? To check on your friend's baby girl?"

Girl.

I don't have to glance at Rhys to know the likely disapproval in his expression.

Detective Vale is a bargainer, a negotiator. Men like him, in his position, use manipulative tactics to get what they want. It's dangerous to meet on a bargainer's terms; they suss out your weakness and exploit it.

I wonder how many bargains he's made with himself.

"All right," I say, accepting his offer. Right now, for me, the benefit outweighs the danger.

As I follow the detective toward the large ER door, Rhys sidles closer to me. "You're being impulsive. Don't give him a statement here."

"Because I'll be too emotional?" I look at him.

His lips thin, his frown tight. "You sell yourself short," he says, lowering his voice as the detective speaks with reception to have us admitted. "You can be just as emotional as the average person, Hale."

"Maybe so, but I present it differently." A personality glitch I hope will perplex Detective Vale.

The door opens, and the detective makes sure I follow

him into the wing. He holds up a hand as Rhys attempts to step through. "I only need a statement from Ms. Hale at this time, Agent Nolan."

Rhys's expression hardens, and I step between the men to diffuse the situation before it has a chance to escalate. "It's fine, Rhys. I won't be long."

He glances at the detective and then me, but says nothing. I watch him take a seat in the waiting room as the door slides closed, severing my view.

"This way," the detective says.

He directs me past another cop in the hallway to a small, empty room. It's stocked with bandages and harmless medical supplies. There's a metal table and two folding chairs in the center. Either used as a nurse break room, or the detective had them brought in himself.

The difference is decisive.

"Is this your setup?" I ask.

He offers me a seat first, his smile forced. "I suppose we're in a similar line of work. You're used to being the one to ask questions, but—" he slips a black notepad from his blazer inseam "—that's my job today."

So it's like that, is it. I decide this is his setup, and that he's hovering around the hospital, close to Cam's baby, because he has no other leads. I would do the same. The perpetrator went to great lengths to control his kill, not to harm the fetus.

I wonder if Cam's husband is here—whether or not he's the prime suspect.

Detective Vale clicks his pen, initiating the interview. "Ms. Hale, why did you and Agent Nolan come to West Melbourne?"

I slip my bag off my shoulder and anchor the strap

across the chair back. "We're working the Delany cold case," I answer simply, honestly.

He doesn't bother jotting the note. "Was the case selected for you, or do you and Agent Nolan decide which cases to take?"

I flash a curt smile. "Detective, you know I'm not at liberty to discuss the inner workings of the FBI."

He matches my smile with a snide one of his own. "Okay then. Can you tell me if you noticed the similarities between the Delany murder and your attack before you signed on to the case?" He reaches down to a binder and plucks out a manila file.

Marks, Cynthia is written on the tab.

My shoulders tense. I'm not surprised that he connected the similarities. I'm alarmed that he went there so quickly. No preamble.

"You're not one for foreplay," I say. I stole that line from Rhys. He used it on a cop we interviewed on a previous case, and it worked then, just as it's working now.

Detective Vale cocks his head, annoyed. "I like to get to the point. Again, time is of the essence, Ms. Hale. Or should we cut the shit completely and I refer to you as Ms. Marks?"

"Hale is my name now, detective. And no," I say, propping my elbows on the table. "I didn't read the whole case file prior."

The truth.

He looks dubious at my response. "So you're saying that you just blindly accept a case without first knowing all the details?" He shakes his head. "You must trust your partner very much."

"I do. Don't you trust yours?"

His gaze narrows, then he says, "At any time after you arrived in West Melbourne, once you were aware of the Delany case details, did you suspect Agent Nolan chose it because of the similarities to your attack?"

His questions are going to keep getting longer and more detailed until he gets the answer he wants. "Again, I trust my partner. If he'd done such an obtuse thing, he'd have discussed it with me beforehand. What is the baby's name?"

This catches him off guard. "What?"

"Cameron's baby. The name?"

He frowns. "Doesn't have one yet. The husband claims the name they had picked out was her choice, and he can't bring himself to use it now."

Elton. That's her husband's name. The fact that Detective Vale refers to him as "the husband" means Elton is at least a suspect, if not the prime.

"When did you realize the parallels between the cases?" he fires back.

About the time I was staring at my dead friend on an autopsy table.

"Many cases that involve stabbings appear similar," I say. He's like a dog with a bone.

"You don't find it odd or…coincidental that Cameron was killed in nearly the same method that you were attacked?"

I quirk an eyebrow. "Nearly?"

He clears his throat. "Eight stab wounds. The murder weapon was measured to be the same width, inflicting similar lacerations. The only difference is that the victim's abdomen was left undamaged." He pauses a beat. "As I suspect you already know, seeing as you spoke with the ME this morning."

"Is that a question, detective?"

"What were you doing at the medical examiner's office this morning, Ms. Hale?"

"Agent Nolan and I were there to interview Dr. Keller on the Delany case."

His dark eyes hold mine for a second too long, then he flips open my case file. "Would you consider yourself and Cameron Ortega friends?" He switches gears quickly.

I hike an eyebrow. "You mean, *did* I consider us friends before she was murdered?"

"Right."

I sit back. I don't like where he's taking this interview. "We were college friends."

Interrogation trick: Like being on the witness stand in court, never offer more information than what's being asked.

"Cameron's phone records show a text message she sent you with her address, confirming a visit to her home yesterday."

That didn't take him long to discover.

"Were you friends yesterday?" he presses.

"I'd like to think so. People fall away after college. They move on, get married, have a family." I consider this a moment, then: "A friend is someone who gives you total freedom to be yourself."

"What...? Emerson? Nietzsche?"

"Morrison. Jim."

This actually gets a smile from him. "Why did you visit the victim yesterday?"

Two slow breaths. "I'd seen that Cam had moved to

West Melbourne, and that she was expecting. I wanted to catch up with my college friend while in town."

If my phone or computer records are subpoenaed, he'll see where I looked up Cam's social media profile.

He makes a note. "What time did you arrive at the Ortega residence?"

The questioning goes on like this for a few minutes, where he gathers the facts. He repeats the questions, changing up the order and phrasing. A deliberate tactic to make me slip.

But I have nothing to hide; I answer honestly. Until he asks me the one question that makes me hesitate.

"Ms. Hale?" he says, and reiterates the question. "Did you notice anyone else near the residence yesterday?"

The supply room door opens. Rhys walks in, escorted by an officer.

Detective Vale stands. "Why is he here?" He directs this question to the cop in a blue uniform.

"I'm Ms. Hale's representation," Rhys says as he takes up my side.

"You know you can't do that," Detective Vale says.

For the first time, the detective and I are in agreement.

I look up at Rhys in question, demanding an explanation in our silent code.

"I've never officially practiced," Rhys says, planting his hands on the table. "But I have the degree to back it up. From this point on, Ms. Hale will have council present during any interviews."

Detective Vale looks dejected about this development, but he takes his seat, resuming the interrogation. "I'm making some calls. This better check out."

"It will," Rhys assures him.

I sit in stunned silence. *Why didn't he tell me?*

My initial reaction is anger. I feel betrayed. Rhys has always been adamant about being truthful...but in retrospect, that was directed toward me, to open up about my past for my case.

Anger is a defensive reaction to the source. The truth is, I'm hurt.

How much about one another do we really know? Other than our cases, we don't see each other outside of work. I don't have much of a social life in Missouri. And because I'm guarded, I haven't ventured to know anything about him other than he was terminated from fieldwork.

"Do I need to repeat the question?" Detective Vale says.

Rhys kneels beside me so that we're level. He gives me an apologetic smile, but one that says now's not the time—we need to get through this first.

I nod, then direct my attention on Vale. "Yes."

"Did you notice anyone around the Ortega residence yesterday?"

"I'm advising my client not to answer that," Rhys says.

Vale glares across the table, then dips back into my file. "It says here that Torrance Carver was interviewed in connection to your attack." He looks up at me. "Did you recently question Mr. Carver and his brother, Mike Rixon, while investigating the Delany case?"

Rhys lightly brushes my leg beneath the table. "I'm advising my client not to answer."

"Christ," the detective whispers harshly. "Can I assume this is how the rest of the interview will go?"

"Unless you're willing to disclose what your intent is with Ms. Hale, then yes. She has cooperated and has nothing further to say." Rhys stands. "We do have the matter of Joanna Delany's case to discuss, though."

Detective Vale stands to match Rhys. "I'm a little busy with the current murder investigation, but you're welcome to get a copy of my case notes." He pulls out his phone and sends a text. "It will be waiting for you at the precinct."

"We appreciate that," Rhys says.

A thick current of tension hums in the air between Rhys and Vale, regardless of their professional etiquette. I push my chair back, making a loud scraping sound to disturb the silence.

"We'll let you know if we have any questions about the Delany case," I say.

"You do that, Ms. Hale."

Rhys heads to the door, but I don't budge. I look at Detective Vale expectantly.

"Oh right," he says. "Seems that I wasn't authorized to give you visitation, after all."

I grab my bag and hoist it across my shoulder. I could have the last word; I could tell Detective Vale what I think about his interview skills that are completely obvious and lacking. Or the fact that I could smell his unpleasant breath from across the table.

Instead, I offer him a smile and leave. I stop myself from thanking him, as that feels crass. He doesn't need to know that, by trying to intimidate me, he's given us a key piece of his investigation.

Once we're outside the hospital, Rhys says, "I promise, I'll explain. But we need to get the handwriting analyses back from Quantico first so we can—"

"See if either Torrance or his brother is a match to the note," I finish for him.

We stop at the trunk of the rental car, and Rhys studies me. "You caught that."

"I did. Detective Vale is conducting interviews at the hospital. Why? The perpetrator spared Cam's baby. He thinks there's a link to my case."

Rhys nods slowly as he thinks it through. "He's looking at Torrance as the prime suspect. A theory that Cameron could've maintained an affair with him throughout her marriage."

"Right. He's read my file. Read Cam and Torrance's statements. Torrance is connected to both victims. I mean all three…"

Rhys does something so uncharacteristically open, my breath catches. He hooks a finger beneath my chin and lifts my face, angling my gaze to meet his.

"You're not a victim," he says.

I nod against his hand. "I know."

"Do you?" His thumb strokes my cheek, his slate eyes intense, before he drops his hand. He steps away, putting a comfortable distance between us, and I drag in a full breath.

"What I meant was, Torrance has a link to all three women. Me, Cam, and Joanna. With his juvi assault record, that makes him suspect number one."

Rhys looks up at the sky, then checks the time on his phone. "Let's get our answers to the handwriting analyses before Vale brings in Torrance."

"All right."

I appreciate Rhys's collective control. By staying calm and not leaping to conclusions, he's keeping me grounded. We're here to solve Joanna Delany's murder. If, by chance or fate…or some other divine design…we discover a perpetrator to investigate in my attack…

There's time.

First, the cold case.

I was so focused on Drew not having a competent alibi that I failed to connect the other piece of the puzzle. Torrance had gone along with Cam's lie—why? The obvious explanation: He still needed an alibi. Which gave him motive to get rid of Cam—the person who could reveal the truth and implicate him.

As we head to the Tiki Hive, I try to envision Torrance stalking toward me on the dock. His hand gripping a knife. I try to visualize his features on the man who pulled me from the lake. I see the white lotuses on the dark water.

I blink hard when the rest won't come.

If we prove Torrance is the killer, I will have to accept it as fact. Regardless of what my mind wants to believe. There's no room for two beliefs. The mind is the most powerful tool. But just like a tool, it can be sharpened and molded. It can be bent. It can be trained to believe almost anything.

23

BOOK OF DREW

LAKIN: THEN

Have you ever told a lie and immediately regretted it? Either because you believed you're inherently an honest person, or because the lie contradicted your principles, your own beliefs? How badly did you feel after telling the lie? What did you feel? Remorse? Guilt?

This is called cognitive dissonance. The uncomfortable feeling that squirms inside you when two beliefs challenge each other. When this occurs, our mind has to decide how to correct the imbalance and restore harmony. To alleviate the guilt, in other words.

There are four choices:

Modify. Trivialize. Add. Deny.

We can modify our belief system to accept a portion of the lie as truth. Or trivialize it, coming to the conclusion that the outcome of the lie isn't that important. We can add another cognition, or behavior or belief, on top of the lie in order to accept what we've done. Or we can downright deny that we ever told a lie to begin with.

The last one gets a bit tricky.

How do we convince ourselves of something that we fundamentally know is the opposite?

Logically, we have to understand that our mind wants to protect us. If a belief is causing pain, the brain will map a way around that area of hurt in order to find a less painful avenue.

The path of least resistance.

It's why we occasionally look at people and question their choices, their situations. It's inconceivable to us, in our belief structure. But we haven't walked in their shoes, to quote a cliché. We don't know the logical avenues their brain had to map in order to protect them from destruction.

I'm thinking about this now, as I write a scene from my past, because—at this particular moment in time—I couldn't see the path ahead. I wasn't aware of the very real pain my relationship with my psych professor was causing.

Love, in so many ways, is a deceptive lie in itself, triggered by the chemicals in our brain.

Maybe that's a bit jaded. Or maybe it's just plain science.

On this day, Drew was lounging in a hammock on the back lanai of his Spanish Colonial home, book in hand. A mystery novel. Something I'd teased him about; his guilty pleasure.

"You're supposed to be writing a paper," he said, and flipped a page in his book.

I put my pen down on the patio table. "It's coming off as rambly."

He looked over at me. "Rambly?"

I twisted my lips. I'd heard Cam use it recently. "I am a college student, you know."

He set the book on the deck and rocked out of the hammock. "You're not just a college student. If that were the case, I'd have no interest in you."

"Very bluntly put." Tired of this latest head game, I stood and marched toward the house. Lately, Drew and I had been testy with each other. Not fighting. Not even arguing, per se. Just…prickly, for lack of a better word.

Maybe it was the upcoming spring break trip. With less than a week to go, I'd been anxious to get away. From school. From Cam. My parents.

Chelsea.

I sensed Drew behind me, closing in. I sped up as I neared the sliding-glass door. He grabbed me around the waist and lifted me off the deck. I squealed as he slung me around and pinned my back to the glass.

Hair slipped from my bun and covered the side of my face. He cupped the back of my neck, digging in his fingers and tilting my head. He wedged his knee between my thighs and forced them apart, so he could slip his other hand beneath my skirt.

I bit my lip hard, but a deep, achy noise slipped free.

His mouth hovered close to mine as he said, "If you paid closer attention in class, then you'd have Law of effect nailed by now."

I took measured breaths, unable to control the tremor in my voice as his palm grazed my skin and inched higher. Heat simmered from deep within. "Maybe I would, if you'd teach rather than *nailing* your students."

Sharp pain snatched my breath as Drew pinched my inner thigh, hard enough to leave a mark. "*Student*," he stressed. "Maybe you need another lesson in operant conditioning."

I swallowed. "I'm easily distracted," I said, changing course. "My teacher is pretty hot."

But this didn't alleviate the aggressive resentment thrumming through him. Jaw set rigidly, he gripped my face before he kissed me savagely. I gave in to the yearning, the hunger to have him desire me again.

I knew my behavior was causing a rift between us, but I couldn't control the compulsion. I'd been making snide accusations about him and Chelsea. The signs were obvious to me, though. Along with Chelsea's grossly observable flirtation, there was the recurring dream. I was sleep deprived and paranoid. And the gossip inflamed an already tender nerve.

According to the rumor mill, Chelsea's pursuit of the professor was a welcome one; Drew's parents not opposed to the union of their prestigious families.

He broke the kiss. "I only want you."

I searched his eyes, seeking that uncomfortable feeling —that *tell*—which would present with a lie. If he felt guilt, if he was disturbed by it, he hid it well.

Drew's life was—compared to most—a charmed life. Wealthy. Educated. Attractive. He wanted for nothing, and yet he found ways to endanger it all. Like a gambler needed to skirt the brink to feel alive.

"I'm not good for you," I admitted, shocked when it left my mouth. I'd never professed it aloud before, but he had to know it was the truth.

The Chelseas and Drews of the world were better. They just were.

His voice softened. "I only want you," he repeated.

He didn't refute my claim. He couldn't. I knew right then that I could never be his match, his equal, just as I'd known when I was a child that I'd never be like Amber. She shined so brightly…until her light went out. Me trying to exist in his world was like trying to force a square peg into a round hole. Too much friction. It doesn't belong.

"Why?" I had to know. *Why me*?

He smoothed my hair away from my face, his gaze dancing over my features. "It's the human condition. We want what's bad for us. We're designed to self-destruct."

Our bubble burst in that moment. Reality crept in like a thief, stealing my serenity, my bliss I'd found with Drew. He was an excellent teacher. *The Law of effect*. My behavior was earning me unpleasant consequences from him.

Pain, acute and blinding, lanced my soul. I only had four choices:

Modify. Trivialize. Add. Deny.

The lie I told myself was that, if I was incapable of change, then Drew could change. That he would shun his affluent life for me. Because we were special together— neither one of us had ever experienced such intense emotions before.

I was half right.

And when his lips descended on mine, I was well again. The dark tide washing ashore within me started to recede.

Cognitive dissonance ensures that our mind will correct the imbalance.

MURDER BOARD

LAKIN: NOW

"You guys must either really like bar food or—" Mike Rixon breaks off in the middle of his sentence, letting the weight of implication hang heavy in the air.

Rhys picks up on his thread as we approach the bar top. "We have a few more questions for Torrance."

"He's not here," Mike answers simply. "But when I see him, I'll let him know to contact you."

"Thanks," Rhys says. "We also have another question for you, regarding Kohen Hayes."

On our drive here, I examined the handwriting analysis report. These reports read kind of like throwing a dart at a moving target...while amid a tornado. Strong winds send that dart somewhere in the vicinity of the target, but you have to include many other factors in order for it to be useful.

They're best used for ruling people out. Mike Rixon, for example, was ruled out as the author of the note by

94%. His half-brother, Torrance, scored 33%. Considering that's below fifty percent, we can't entirely rule him out, but we can't confirm with one hundred percent accuracy that he did write the note.

Math makes my head hurt.

All we know for sure is that Torrance scored lower than his brother, and Torrance is the only one of our persons of interest who has a connection linking him to all three women.

That makes Torrance our prime suspect for the time being, and the local authorities—particularly Detective Vale—are already interested in him. Once major crimes gets him into an interrogation box, our cold case will be sidelined.

My case will be sidelined.

And Cam...

I try to keep perspective, but as I stand here, anxiously twirling the band around my wrist, watching Rhys suss out the truth from Mike about why Kohen was fired, I feel as if the walls are starting to close in.

"I need some air," I say to Rhys, as I'm already bolting for the open doors of the bar.

Rhys cuts his conversation short and follows me outside.

The sprawling beach deck is teeming with beach goers as they crowd in for the lunchtime rush. The crashing waves of the ocean sound too loud in my ears, all other noise muffled and distant against the battering wind.

"Hale, wait."

It's Rhys's voice that finds me, and I brace my back against one of the beams.

"Just breathe," he says.

He lets me get through the sudden anxiety attack on my own, giving the adrenaline time to work its way out of my system. A person can only panic for so long. After about ten minutes, the mind and body regulates. You just have to keep your composure until the attack passes.

Rhys moves in closer, blocking most of the people from my view. "Better?"

I nod. "It's just…all catching up. Or hitting too fast at once." I'm embarrassed. I don't suffer panic attacks. This isn't common.

However, when it comes to Rhys, I don't need to elaborate. The concern etched in hard creases on his face softens with his understanding. "You haven't had time to process Cam," he says knowingly. "Or mourn her."

It's only been hours, but it feels longer, *much* longer since I saw her body on the slab. I cringe at my internal thoughts. I'm not even sentimental in the privacy of my mind.

"Process," I repeat as the events catch up. "Like the fact that my partner is apparently a lawyer."

Rhys sighs. "Come on." He attempts to guide me to the boardwalk without touching my arm.

He leads me toward the shore, where low tide leaves a crescent of paved sand. Without a word, he plunks down a few feet away from the cresting waves, a silent request for me to do the same.

I seat myself beside him, trying to ignore the feel of wet sand as saltwater seeps into my slacks.

"Truth has a way of coming out," he says. He stares out over the ocean; won't meet my eyes. I wonder if he's thinking about the note I kept from him in that statement. "I should've handled that better."

A sudden surge of guilt steals over me. We all have secrets. "It's not really any of my business. I was just... surprised. You never mentioned it."

Rhys picks up a lone sea oat shoot and scrapes the hard-packed sand. "No, it's fair. I've plundered through your life, asking the hard questions. Least I could do was tell you a piece of mine."

To be really fair, I came to him asking for help on my case. I invited him to plunder into my life. "Parents?" I ask generally.

His tight smile doesn't reach his eyes. "You'd make a good profiler. Yeah, my dad. I come from a family of lawyers. I'm the middle son, and when I changed course to the FBI, my dad wasn't too thrilled."

"You have to be in the field." I can't picture Rhys in a courtroom.

"The getting shot part didn't go over too well with him, either. It was like I proved him right; that I wouldn't make it as a field agent. I even thought about returning to the law during my rehabilitation leave."

I rest my hand on his forearm. A foreign show of emotion, of empathy, but with Rhys, it feels natural. I want to offer him comfort.

"Why didn't you?"

He looks at me, covers my hand with his. "You."

A gust of wind steals my breath. I inhale deeply, filling my lungs. "Rhys..."

"You wouldn't leave me alone," he says with a curt laugh. "So I told myself I'd take one more case, then retire. But we know how that actually turned out."

I recall how moody he was when I first spoke with him. At times, I still see a glimpse of the sullen anger that lurks within him over his injury, over being taken out of the field. But… "I needed you. I couldn't have gotten this far without you," I say honestly.

There is no hesitancy in his gaze as he searches my face. Whether it's my admission of needing him that's shocked him silent, or something else…

He glances down at our hands, still touching. Then he turns mine over, exposing the rubber band. His thumb probes the delicate skin beneath the band, the rough pad of his thumb an arousing friction against the red, sensitized skin.

"I wish you wouldn't cause yourself pain," he says.

The urge to pull my wrist away thrums through me with violent need, but I don't move. "It was part of my therapy," I admit. "I just became conditioned to it, I guess."

"Dr. Lauren?" he asks. He had to interview her while he was in Silver Lake working my cold case. She couldn't divulge anything that would break patient-doctor confidentiality, but she confirmed my memory loss, my battle with physical recovery.

I nod in confirmation. "It distracted me from the pain. Whenever the rehabilitation therapy would become too much, she said to snap the band. My mind would focus on that sudden, sharp pain, giving my body a reprieve. If only for a moment."

Something flashes in his eyes; a realization. Maybe Rhys understands more than most about needing an interruption from the pain.

He's still holding my hand, his thumb absently tracing my wrist. Another blast of wind sends my hair across my face and, as I pull away to clear it from my eyes, he reaches up and tucks the strands behind my ear.

His hand lingers there, the tips of his fingers lightly touching my jaw. I think again of that moment at the lake, when he kissed my forehead. And of last night, when the question of us charged the air—when all I had to do was move closer.

His tie flaps against his arm in the breeze, and I imagine a braver version of myself grabbing hold of it and bringing his mouth crashing against mine. As his gaze settles on my lips, I part my mouth in anticipation, wondering if he's envisioning the same.

If time would just slow down long enough to let me make a choice…

Before I can will my body to act, he blinks and turns toward the ocean. Drops his hand from my face. He breaks the connection, and a knot tightens in my stomach.

"A reprieve," he says, picking up the thin shoot again. "Like an intermission." He draws a diagonal line in the sand.

"What?"

"What is that psychology term you always talk about? When the mind can't harbor two beliefs at once?"

I blink against the wind, willing my brain to transition. "Cognitive dissonance?"

"Right. What if the killer is experiencing something like that?" He now draws three vertical lines off the main line. "Let's imagine there are no other victims out there. That our guy isn't a serial killer. His victimology has purpose. Maybe he's feeling some form of guilt; that's why he spared Cam's baby. You were targeted first—" he breaks off as he scrawls my name along one line "—then

Joanna. Then Cameron. If the cases are linked, then Joanna had to have had some connection to the both of you."

If the cases are linked. With everything we've discovered, with all the similarities, we still have to be objective. "I didn't know her. She was younger than me. We didn't grow up in the same area or attend the same school." I contemplate this for a moment. "And I don't think Cam would've known her, either."

Rhys scores out five more lines. Then, along each writes: Torrance, Mike, Kohen, Drew, Chelsea. He's created a murder board in the sand.

All suspects, but the last name gives me pause. "How is Chelsea factored in?"

"Did you ever consider Chelsea for the author of the note?"

I shake my head. "No. I mean, the very first letter… The first time I read it, I assumed it was from my attacker."

"Can you remember what it said?"

I can't forget. I read the sick letter over and over, punishing myself, believing that I somehow deserved my fate. I had escaped death, but the author of the note knew I wasn't really alive. My attacker stole much more than my security, my right to exert safety. They sucked away precious moments of my life, stole time away from me.

Then with the note…it was a promise to finish what was started.

I recite the letter word for word to Rhys, watching as his face gets that serious expression when he's deep in thought. "Does that sound like a woman could've penned it?"

He flicks wet sand with the tip of the reed. "I'm not

sure," he says. "We're looking for a nexus with the victims. Chelsea knows you and Cam, and I imagine, from what I recall, that she was into the glamorous scene. She might've known Joanna from her modeling days."

That's a huge leap. But the only connection to the victims that makes sense so far. But: "You think Chelsea could be good for this?" I had my issues with her—college issues; boyfriend issues—but I never seriously considered her capable of murder.

To me, she was always too vapid.

Never underestimate anyone.

Rhys told me this during our first cold case. And yet, I still can't reconcile it. Because I'm too close to it. I'm not objective, the way Rhys is.

He drops the reed and dusts off his hands on his slacks. "Remorse," he answers simply. "Not saying that our perp isn't psychopathic in nature, but to purposely try *not* to harm Cam's baby, there had to be some measure of remorse during the action. As if her murder was out of necessity rather than victim selection. So our perp has a method, and a purpose. None of this is random." He looks at me. "That is, if the cases are connected."

There's one thing missing—one very big void: *me.* "What necessity would my murder serve?"

He stares at the cresting waves as the tide washes in. "That's the question."

"We need to interview Drew." Logically, this is the next step. Linking the cases. Cam changed her statement, making Drew the only one who can either corroborate or contradict it. He's the one who supplied Chelsea's alibi.

When I press Rhys on contacting Drew, he clears his throat and stands. Offers me his hand. "Not yet. I have to think some things through." I take his hand, and he helps me up beside him. "Why don't you head back to the hotel. Are you okay to drive?"

I step up on the boardwalk and halt, turning to face him abruptly. "Where are you going?"

"I'm going to lean harder on Rixon. Try to get him talking about where Torrance is, or find out if they had any connection to Chelsea, before Vale catches up with him. Rixon might know more about his brother than he lets on."

It's a good plan. Getting to Torrance first with our questions will help our case. Still, there's a tremor of unease in the salt air.

Rhys is keeping something from me.

He sinks his hands into his pockets. "I think…we should get another writing sample."

I agree. "We need samples from everyone."

"No. We need the note, Hale. The one you received before you left Silver Lake."

"I can't get it," I admit. "I destroyed it." But, just as I seared the words into memory, I know the handwriting is a possible match. "I'm almost certain the author wrote both notes," I tell Rhys with assurance.

Rhys looks hesitant, but he trusts me. He's never *not* trusted me, which makes the fact that I know he's keeping a piece from me even more painful.

"I'll meet you at the hotel in a couple of hours," he says, turning to head back into the Tiki Hive.

"Sounds good."

He looks uncertain before he makes the final decision to leave, but he does. He gives me the car keys and enough time to launch my own investigation.

Rhys is a protector by nature. He may be only

temporarily keeping information back because he believes he can spare me some hurt—but that's not how partnerships work.

As I approach the sedan, I see a folded slip of paper tucked beneath the windshield wiper. Dread rears; it's not a parking ticket. I go to snap the band, but stop myself. I face this head-on.

I unfold the letter.

Meet me.

The notes are becoming shorter, more direct. The author is losing patience.

Seated behind the wheel, I think about Rhys's murder board in the sand. The waves washing it away, out of existence. Locating my own answers is just as time sensitive.

25

EMERGENCE

LAKIN: NOW

I'm parked across the street from a beautiful Spanish Colonial.

It was always his favorite style.

My sweat-slicked hands feel slippery on the wheel as I stare at the house. Two figures move behind the lattice fencing of the side patio.

I haven't seen him since...

When was the last time? I've seen images of him online, pictures taken by reporters when he was being questioned in connection to the investigation. But when was the last time I really *saw* him?

The evening of the fight.

The day Chelsea showed up at his door.

Drew didn't visit me in the hospital. By the time I was coherent, he was a suspect—the prime suspect. Logically, his lawyers didn't want him near me. Still, I always found that to be one of his harshest treatments of me; I was dead to him.

But does that make him a killer?

In a theoretical, cosmic sense, we are all killers. One could argue the philosophy of the butterfly effect, where every action has a reaction—cause and effect. I could take the wrong turn at a light and inadvertently derail someone, thereby sending some other soul on the wrong course, creating a chain reaction that would cause the death of another person.

In this case, we're all empiricists, our knowledge of the world gleaned by experience. We're unaware of our participation in said death. It's too distant, abstract. Then there is the individual who goes against the natural order and decides to take fate into their own hands by committing the act of murder. This person wants the experience firsthand. They crave control, over their life and the lives of others.

And that's why I'm here. Now.

To take back control.

I need to know just how complicit Drew was in my murder.

Did my illicit affair with my professor initiate a chain reaction that resulted with me at the bottom of a lake—or was it the sole choice of one person?

To know the truth of Drew, I need to look into his eyes —something I've avoided these past few years—like I look into the eyes of every suspect in every case, and know that I'm looking into the eyes of a killer.

I remove the keys from the ignition and open the car door. Hand clutched into a fist, I slat each key between my fingers, creating a prong-like weapon. A means of defense should something go awry. Rhys caries a service piece. We're always in the field together. He's trained me in self-defense, but venturing into this situation solo, I feel as if I'm walking up to Drew's house exposed, vulnerable.

As I cross the street, my heart rockets to my throat. I feel each step pulse through my veins, a resounding beat in my ears, muffling the world. I walk up the long driveway, and a wave of déjà vu sweeps over me.

I push the unease away and head around the side of the house. Chelsea sees me first.

She's still just as stunning as the last time I laid eyes on her. Long blond waves of hair, golden tan. To be honest, I'm a bit surprised they're still an item. But then they have a child together. No matter Drew's promiscuity, they'd try to make their relationship work. It's what his family would expect of him.

Her eyes grow wide as recognition dawns. "Oh my, God, Drew. That psycho is back. Quick, call the cops."

My steps falter. I grip the keys tighter, shock branching through my stiff limbs. "What?"

Drew is there by her side, taking up all the air as he always did. His presence is consuming, and I'm once again just a pathetic, smitten college girl standing before her professor.

Until he talks.

"Cynthia?"

Incensed at hearing my given name in his snide tone, I snap out of my confused daze. "I'm here to ask some questions," I say, my gaze flitting from Drew to Chelsea. She's latched on to his arm, looking shaken.

Drew's surprise wears off quickly. "What is it now? First that damn FBI agent shows up, now you."

My eyebrows draw together at this. When would Rhys have time… Then it resonates. Rhys went to Quantico. Alone. No—he came here. To see Drew. *Why?*

"Agent Nolan?" I ask, to verify my suspicion.

Drew steps in front of Chelsea. "Yeah. He hasn't left me alone in years. And now I'm going to tell you the same thing I've told him." He takes a step closer. "Leave me the fuck alone."

The keys jangle loose in my hand. I stare down at the green, spongy grass. Rich grass. The kind you purchase as sod. I can make out the divots where the patches were spliced together.

When I glance around, I realize there's something missing from their picturesque life. It niggles at the back of my mind. Where are the toys? The trail of chaos that comes from chasing a toddler?

Where is the toddler?

I rein in my errant thoughts. "What did Agent Nolan ask you?"

Drew's features—that are markedly aged—crease in irritation. He drags a hand through his close-cropped hair, relenting. "Something about another girl that was murdered. Every time there's anything remotely involving a young girl's death, Agent Nolan is barking at my door. He's worse than fucking Dutton was."

His fury strikes me like a whip. "Did you know the victim?" I press. It's hard to get a read on someone when they're angry. It's such a one-sided emotion. No range. Also, I knew him. Had deep feelings for him. I was easily swayed by his manipulation.

That's not something that goes away over time.

If his rage is the only emotion I have to go on, then so

be it. I'll make Drew fume until he gives me what I came here for.

The truth.

I used to get under his skin, too.

"I didn't know her," he says. "Besides. Like I told that agent, I have an alibi. Case closed."

I nod a couple of times. "Cases are so easily closed for you. Out of sight, out of mind."

This seems to dent his armor. "Look, I'm sorry for what happened to you, Cynthia. I really am. But it was a long time ago. You need to move on." He glances at Chelsea, then says, "You need to *let us* move on."

I cock my head. "Where were you yesterday evening?" I demand.

Cam's murder hasn't been made public yet. I shift my focus from Drew to Chelsea, analyzing their responses. Chelsea shakes her head unreliably. Drew simply holds up a hand.

"Enough," he says. "I don't know why you're here, but we're done. With all of this."

"When was the last time you saw or spoke to Cameron?" I force the conversation. When he remains silent, I add, "She was murdered, Drew."

Chelsea gasps. "Oh my, God. Get her out of here."

Arms crossed over his chest, Drew stares at the ground. "Christ," he breathes. His distressed wife to his right clings to him, demanding I be removed from the premises.

Drew finally concedes. "Look, you're upsetting her. You have to leave."

"You slept with Cam."

Chelsea's frail state evaporates on impact of this news. "God, Drew. Did you get her pregnant, too?"

"What?" Drew turns toward her. "No! This is bullshit."

I'm not done. "Where is your child?"

She looks at me as if I've asked the most preposterous question. Unease burrows deep inside, beneath my rib cage. The baby was the inciting incident. It was the first domino tipped. Why is it so outlandish that I would insist on proof of the thing that tore my life apart?

I raise my eyebrows at her, and Chelsea's bravado shifts.

She's *scared* of me. What have I ever done to this woman to warrant this level of fear?

"Where is the baby?" I demand.

My white, sleeveless blouse sticks to my back in the humidity. I'm glad I took my suit jacket off in the car. As the moisture thickens the air with the threat of rain, I'm one thundering heat wave away from passing out.

Drew steps forward, but it's Chelsea who finally answers. "You lost it," she says. "Remember?"

No... No, I do not remember. What is this devil with a golden halo of hair saying? "What are you talking about? I'm asking where the hell you and Drew's kid is. The whole reason why we broke up? Fought that day? And I ended up in the path of a killer?"

I know; this logic goes against everything I've learned and accepted over the past few years. I can't point the finger at Chelsea any more than I can point the finger at Drew for the events that led to my death.

Or can I?

A rush of anger assaults me, and suddenly the heat is boiling my blood.

"Just answer me!"

Drew's features melt into sympathy, and that only makes me seethe more. "I think you're confused, Cynthia."

Now Chelsea: "You were the one that came to Drew's that day," she says. "You told me you were carrying his baby. You were upset. It caused a huge fight."

The world is spinning in the wrong direction.

Drew: "You lost the baby," he says, repeating Chelsea's words. "I'm sorry, Cynthia."

I hold out my hand, as if I can stop the barrage. The keys clang together noisily in my ears. A roar floods my head, and pressure builds...

I close my eyes to stop the sway. That day comes back with biting clarity. The emergence of a memory. The driveway. The mahogany door. My Guess Wedges.

No—not mine. I didn't wear those kinds of shoes. Chelsea wore them.

Like a mirror being flipped, the memory inverts.

Me walking up the driveway, ringing the doorbell. Chelsea answering the door. Drew tracking me down at my apartment. The cops being sent.

The baby.

My baby.

I was only a few weeks pregnant.

I'd just found out that morning.

You lost the baby.

I didn't lose the baby; it was taken.

My hands go to my belly. My fingers find the scars. "Oh, God..."

"Drew, she's crazy. Call someone."

Chelsea's voice bombards my eardrums, and yes, I'm

crazy. I'm *mad*. I'm seconds away from losing all touch with reality. My peripheral wavers, blackening at the edges.

I have to leave.

I have to get safe.

My feet are taking me to the car, although I can't remember moving. Time is skipping. The sordid truth is circling my mind like a murky drain, seeking a way out, an escape.

I ease behind the wheel and, when I calm my erratic breathing, I snap the band around my wrist to center myself. I feel the sting. I blink away the wetness from my eyes. Then I crank the car.

Drew and Chelsea watch me drive away. I glimpse them one last time in the review mirror before I focus on the road ahead.

The first drops of rain plink the windshield.

The rain has finally come.

26

DOWNPOUR

LAKIN: NOW

Silver Lake Memorial is forty-five minutes away from Drew's new home. I don't need the sedan's navigation to direct me there, but I programmed the route anyway. The robotic voice dictating directions is a strange comfort. Keeping me from getting lost in my own thoughts.

Every time I gain a moment of composure, I fall into a memory: Drew's echoing voice bouncing around the lecture hall. His lecture on false memory.

The phenomenon is more common than most think. Especially for trauma patients. I can recite the textbook definition word for word. I know it's real…and yet, I'm struggling to accept false memory as what's happened to me.

I need verifiable proof.

A hospital file directly from the source. Not one doctored to keep a secret.

Because that's the only explanation that I can reason.

Before I make that painful call to my parents, I want proof. Like a good detective needs evidence before they issue an arrest, I have to have chain of evidence in place. And my prime suspect pinned without doubt.

As I stand at the entrance to the hospital, the rain beats down, drenching my clothes. My phone vibrates in my jacket pocket, and I wipe the soaked strands from my face as I pull the phone free.

Rhys's name illuminates the dark screen.

A hollow ache collects around my heart. I send the call to voicemail and walk through the glass doors.

By the time the receptionist has paged the doctor to meet with me, I've worked myself into an emotional state to match my wrecked appearance. For me, that's a rare state, and I'm trembling when Dr. Lawrence approaches.

"Do you remember me?" I ask.

Dark hair streaked with silver, bronzed skin lacking the wrinkles to match his age, he's just as I remember him. That memory is unaffected.

He tilts his head, studying me. "I do, Ms. Marks. How can I help you?"

I swallow the ache. "Why did you doctor the hospital file of my attack? Who asked you to do it?"

I learned this technique from Rhys. Most people want to tell the truth, if you give them a way to pass the blame. Ask the question you want answered, then show them the way to deny culpability.

For Dr. Lawrence, this tactic may not work. His intelligent gaze narrows in confusion. "I'm sorry, but I'm not sure what—"

"I was pregnant at the time of my attack," I interrupt.

"When I recovered, I wasn't. I've read my chart. Many times. There is no mention of a pregnancy." *Tell me I'm not crazy*. "So, I was either pregnant, or I wasn't. Which one is it?"

His sigh stretches out between us. "Ms. Marks, I'm a healer. I took an oath to do no harm. However, you have to understand that sometimes, the line of what constitutes as harm can blur." He waves his hand, ushering me toward a bank of seats.

When we're out of earshot from the hospital staff, he continues. "After your parents consulted with a psychologist, they felt it was in your best interest, for your state of mind, not to know the details of the pregnancy right away."

The pregnancy... Fear confirmed, my lungs cease to accept air for a brief moment.

"As you weren't far along," he says, "I presumed you may not have even known about the baby. But—" he stresses "—I was told that you'd be made aware during rehabilitation. So yes, I went along with another doctor's recommendation based on your mental sate and recovery. But I did not doctor your file, nor did I recommend that your parents keep this from you."

I shake my head. "But Detective Dutton? Wouldn't he have to know the truth? For the investigation?"

His kind eyes darken. "As you were my patient, the only details the case workers were privy to were the ones we discussed beforehand."

Hell. Doctors are not law enforcement. They don't think in terms of motive. Without the knowledge of my pregnancy, I couldn't agree to the detective learning of the baby.

It's a deplorable catch twenty-two banded in red tape.

Dr. Lawrence cups my shoulder. "I can have your original file sent to you via email, if you'd like. Just fill out a request form with Julia at reception."

My parents impeded the investigation. By keeping the pregnancy from Detective Dutton, they inadvertently hid a motive for my murder.

But no matter how upset I am with them, when I leave Silver Lake Memorial, there's only one person I want answers from.

❦

The rental car idles in the hotel parking lot. The heater vents on low, fogging the windows, as rain sheets down the windshield. Outside is dismal and gray, masking the sky in an inky cloud coverage that makes it feel later than the clock reads: 7:24 p.m.

I'm afraid to leave the safe confines of the car. So much has transpired, has been revealed… Has it really only been a day?

Again, time seems to mock me.

Rhys has called three times. Left three messages. I haven't checked them, fearful that the familiar, trustful sound of his voice will weaken me further. Somewhere between the drive from the hospital to the hotel, the anger —completely justified anger—I felt toward him ebbed, as if the storm stole my thunder.

Now I'm damp, cold, hungry, and just…exhausted.

I want to curl up in the hotel bed sheets and blot out the world and all its misery—but that means facing Rhys.

And I'm just not that strong right now.

I turn off the engine and recline the seat, deciding to sleep right here in the car. Only my mind churns details of my case like the raging storm outside the car, keeping me awake.

This is the reality I didn't want to confront yet. I haven't reconciled the loss of a child I will never again be able to have. Not only did my killer take that baby away, they took away any future chance of being a mother.

That pain is far too acute to feel in this moment.

I'm scared I'll stop breathing.

Instead, I pull from the depth of my anger, latch on to that spite, and dig in my heels. Anger is the easiest emotion to govern when reaching for control. I think of the murder board I covered, of the names branched from the event.

I want to believe that a secret this monumental would be impossible to keep—and yet, I know that to be untrue. The darkest, most shattering secrets are the ones that are begged to be kept, even when they're slowly killing you.

So, who all knew? Who was able to keep a secret like this?

My parents. The ones who convinced my doctor to honor doctor-patient confidentiality.

Drew. Who would not breathe a word of the pregnancy. Makes sense. Most likely his lawyers instructed him that a forgotten pregnancy was the best thing that could've happened to him.

Chelsea. Who, in order to support her future husband, would have no qualms in denying any rumors of a pregnancy. Less scandal to contend with.

Cameron. Did she know?

I search my memory bank. The hours surrounding my death are still fuzzy, and I can't trust any recovered memories.

If Cam knew, she took that secret to her grave. Maybe that's why she was nervous when I was at her home, demanding she tell me about the day in the hospital.

A pang of guilt resonates deeply. Maybe if she'd told me long before this point, I could've protected her. She might still be alive.

Now, I can't ask her.

But the question remains: Does Rhys know?

Maybe my parents and the doctor and those being looked at during the investigation could keep this a secret from the Leesburg PD—but I find it impossible to believe they could hide it from an FBI agent.

With a resigned breath, I open my eyes and dig out my phone, stare at the dark display. I'd rather look into Rhys's eyes when I ask my questions, but I'm scared I'll falter—that he'll use some rationality to try to defend himself...or he won't defend himself at all. I'm not sure which would hurt worse.

I open my call log and tap his name just as a knock sounds on the window.

My heart rams my chest, and I drop the phone.

Rhys stands on the other side of the fogged glass. "Hale, Christ. Where have you been?"

I clutch the phone and, all fear replaced with the wrenching pain of betrayal, I shove the door open. He quickly backs out of the way.

The rain falls straight down in heavy pellets. His dress shirt is soaked, his wet hair matted and darkened by rain.

He's my partner. He's my friend. He's beautiful...the one person I let myself trust after the attack, and the doubt I see brimming in his slate eyes kills me.

Rhys is an expert at reading people. He's reading me now. "You went to see Drew."

I don't answer. I want to ask the questions. "You knew I was pregnant." Not a question. I just need to hear him admit the truth.

His lips thin, rivulets of rainwater drip down his face. "Yes."

"All this time..." I trail off, the ache burning my throat. "You led me to believe that Drew had no motive. But you kept looking at him, didn't you? He was always your number one suspect."

He nods slowly. "Yes," he says again. "I kept looking at him."

His clipped, direct answers infuriate me further. "How could you keep this from me?"

He swallows hard, throat dipping with the force. "When I came down here the first time, I spoke with your therapist. She felt your memory loss was your mind's way of protecting you."

Not *loss*—false memory. I didn't just forget I was pregnant; I built a whole other memory, trading places with Chelsea. That's an even worse punishment.

"And I agreed that telling you wouldn't further the investigation," he continues. "It would only hurt you and might set you back psychologically. It wouldn't change anything."

Each breath is a sharp object scraping my chest. "It changes *every*thing."

He pushes a hand through his wet hair. "I tried to tell you, Lakin. I did. So many times. But I just…couldn't."

I blink against the rain, letting the memory resurface. Rhys took me to the Dock House to try to jog my memory of the attack, yes, but there was more to it. He wanted me to remember the pregnancy. That was the sadness I saw in his eyes that night. The reason he kissed me, comforted me.

His guilt.

"You tried to make me relive my murder so that you wouldn't feel guilty over keeping such a vital secret from me," I say, as the realization occurs. "Every day that we worked together, every day that you looked me in the eyes… and just *knew*. You kept a piece of me from myself, Rhys."

His gaze flares as he steps forward. "Just like you hid the note from me?"

Insult wounds deep. "No. No—you do not get to flip this around on me. You let me believe a lie!"

He moves in closer. "I was wrong. Okay? I admit it. I should've told you that night on the lake. I'm wrong for being too weak, not strong enough to bear your pain. I was selfish. But, dammit, so were you. You kept the note hidden. Did it ever occur to you that *that* might be a vital piece of the investigation?"

I shake my head, then turn away. "I'm done, Rhys."

He stops me. His hand circles my arm, forcing me to face him. "You thought it was from him."

The accusation in his tone affronts me. I can only stare up at him. Shocked. Wounded. "Do not go there." I try to pull my arm free, but his hold is stone. "I can't believe this. You never acknowledge that my hallucination is anything but. Now you want to bring it up and weaponize it, to use it against me?"

"That first note…," he says. His voice lowers as his grip softens. "Yes, it could've been from the perp. But if analyzed another way, could've been from a witness. I know who you're waiting for. The man you believe saved you, Lakin. You write about him. Think about him. You dream about him. Real or fiction, it doesn't matter to you. You've shut yourself off completely. Only one man—this hero you've conjured—is good enough."

"What? Are you jealous?" How did this argument get so derailed? "Stop twisting things. You lied to me. What's more, how can you even say this to me? How can you judge me? Knowing what I've suffered? What I now know was taken…"

For the second time today, I feel the fiery ache of tears sting my eyes, and I release a harsh curse. All these years, all the torment, and not one single drop. Now, in the rain, the dam bursts.

Rhys sees past the rain, sees down to my marrow. He places his hand on my cheek, letting his thumb trace the track of tears.

"I'm not judging you. I'm judging myself." His other hand cups my face, holding me too close to him. Where I can't escape. "I never closed your case. It's not a cold case to me; it's always active. I'm always working it. Damn right I'm jealous of him. Because I want to be the one who saves you."

My heart drums. "Rhys…"

The storm has come. We're standing amid the fury of it. Our gazes lock, that dare we've been dancing around simmering the air between us, challenging one of us to take the risk. Rain sheets down in a torrent equal to the thunder resounding inside me, my pulse an electric web of lightning striking and setting my blood aflame. I'm pulled under the swell as his mouth descends on mine, rendering me powerless, *his*.

𝕾 27 𝕾

COLLIDE

LAKIN: NOW

Rhys doesn't kiss me; he consumes me. Devouring any barrier in his way.

The air around us, the oxygen in my lungs, the atoms we're made of. Every molecule implodes into that kiss, and I'm a part of the undertow pulling us beneath the current. I latch on to him, my hands seeking to anchor me to his solid embrace.

His lips make a study of mine, as if he's wanted to explore this forbidden question between us for far too long, and now he's desperate for the answer.

My thighs hit the car behind us, and Rhys lifts me up against him, seating me on the hood to get better access to all of me. I tug at his wet shirt, gripping the collar to bring him closer.

Too soon, he pulls away, breaking the kiss. "Don't," I whisper. I can't conjure any other words. He just can't stop, because I'm scared to let our logical minds catch up with our hearts.

He rests his forehead to mine, easing out a breath. "I never meant to hurt you," he says. I can hear the anguish in his voice, and I believe him. Still...

I'm fighting my desire for him and my need to know. "Then why?"

"I didn't trust myself," he admits. I pull my swollen lip between my teeth, and Rhys answers my unspoken question. "I couldn't keep the truth from you forever, I knew that. But once I knew the truth, I became obsessed with finding evidence to prove it was Abbot, and that's why I couldn't be the one to tell you—I didn't want you to suffer that same devastating frustration."

What's worse than never solving a cold case and finding the killer? Finding the killer and watching him roam free.

Rhys and I both understand this. I know that, in our profession and as partners, as friends, his protective nature wanted to shield me from a dark rabbit hole, but: "I'm stronger than you think, Rhys."

He cups my face, the rain becoming a mist around us. "I know you're strong. My failure has nothing to do with the way I see you, Lakin. This is my weakness; you're my weakness. There would've been no way for me to keep a professional distance from you if I had to watch you break."

Now that his words are out there, and we've proven the professional distance between us has disintegrated—what does it mean? Is he simply filling the void after his own accident? Or does the discovery of my shattering truth do just as he claims: make it impossible for him not to feel for me?

What will we feel tomorrow if we cross this line?

An anxious flutter bats to life in my chest. "Is this some kind of lawyer logic?" A rare smile twitches at my lips.

With Rhys, I never have to pretend to know how to respond to a torrent of emotion. I can feel the overwhelm and process it in my own way, and he allows me this. Always accepting.

His answer is a deep and sensuous kiss that steals my breath, making me forget, for just a moment, the cruel truth of my past. The parking lot vanishes. The rain isn't a burden. We're within our own world, safe. Sheltered.

And when the kiss leads us inside his hotel room, our drenched clothes peeled from our bodies in urgent need to be closer, skin-to-skin, I don't fight the tide. I let the rush of emotions break through every defense. Rhys's touch sears me in a way that chases my darkest fears away.

Right now, Rhys is the light I want to cling to, to reach for.

Our soaked clothes pooled on the floor around us, I stand before him bare and vulnerable. The dim nightlight of the bathroom exposes every scar on my flesh. The ache to close my eyes and hide from this moment stirs beneath my skin, the scar slashed across my chest an enflamed ember of doubt.

But my eyes remain open, even when I start to tremble. I let my gaze roam over Rhys. His scored body mirrors my own. The wounds he's suffered in the field as an agent, the damage he sustained to his leg. The white scar drags down his thigh; the multiple operations to correct the injury.

He takes me by the nape, closing the distance between us. His coarse palm trails my neck, feeling his way over my shoulder, casting rising gooseflesh along my skin. He maps a path down my arm...stopping when he reaches the rubber band that always shackles my wrist.

His finger dips beneath the thin band, he drags it over my hand. "Tonight, with me, you won't need this," he says. As he sinks to his knees, his hands cup my hips.

I try for even breaths, but they're ragged and clipped as they escape. I let my hands rest on his shoulders as he tenderly kisses my belly, my chest, my scars. One by one, every scar he memorized working my cold case, he caresses affectionately, lovingly.

The acceptance of our bodies, of our pain—this is the only way for us to make love.

I lower myself before him, draping my legs around his hips as he seats himself on the floor. We move fluidly together, like a dance that guts you to watch, it's so beautiful. We make love on the hotel room floor. We fuck in the bed on top of the tacky floral bedspread. And when Rhys notices the pain breaking through, my mind wandering to what was stolen from me, and every betrayal I've uncovered...he won't allow it to tear into our night. He makes love to me again. And again. Until I'm too spent to think.

We become a tangle of languid limbs on the bed. I don't know what time it is, and I don't want to know.

We talk about the revelations of the case. We're still partners; this comes naturally to us. In this sense, nothing has changed. I still feel as open as ever with Rhys, even while his thumb traces the lines of my palm.

"Did you locate Torrance?" I ask.

Rhys stirs next to me. "No. I felt like Rixon was putting me off." He exhales heavily. "I wanted to ask Torrance about his knowledge of you and the pregnancy. Try to nail down why he lied to the police about being with Cam."

That's why he sent me away. I think about that for a second, trying to string together Rhys's logic on the two cases now knowing what he does about me: the baby, and Drew. "But you're still looking at Drew."

He squeezes my hand reassuringly. "Torrance can confirm what Cameron told you, giving us an opening to question Drew's alibi. Was he with Cam the whole time during your attack?" He shakes his head against the pillow. "I wish we could question Cameron."

"That's precisely the reason why we can't," I say, letting the sick realization take root. "Someone followed me to her, and that same person wants both cases to go away."

Rhys turns to look at me. "How did Chelsea respond to you when you confronted Drew?"

I wish I could void that one memory. "She was frightened of me." *But was it an act?*

Cam admitted she was with Drew that night after she left the Dock House, which means Chelsea has no alibi. Drew used Chelsea as his alibi to keep his and Cam's relationship a secret. But if all parties were clandestinely together...where was Chelsea during the attack?

I sit up in bed. *The note.*

With the events of the day, I forgot about the newest letter. I climb out of bed and dig it out from my pants pocket. The folded page is wet, the paper is welded together. "Shit."

"What is it?" Rhys asks, now alert.

I fill him in on where I located the note and what it said. I lay it on the table to dry, hoping it's salvageable. "The author thinks it's time for us to meet," I say.

"That would not be good, Lakin. Putting you on their terms."

I nod. "I know this. I honestly thought it was another attempt to scare me away." But the timing. Who followed us to the Tiki Hive? "Chelsea would've had just enough time to deliver the note and rush home before I showed up there." It's plausible, but... "Is the author of the note the killer?"

Rhys runs a hand through his disheveled hair. "Not to sound sexist, but I never looked too hard at Chelsea, because that level of sadistic revenge falls too outside the profile of a woman murderer. To kill a mother and her unborn baby…that's highly atypical."

Atypical or not, it gives her motive. How badly did she want me out of Drew's life?

"But if Chelsea sent the first note, it could be theorized that, after a failed attempt to get rid of you and the pregnancy, she wanted to scare you away."

I crawl into bed and lay next to Rhys. I rest my hand on his bare chest. "We'll look into her harder. Tomorrow."

He kisses the top of my head, and it feels so natural. This new ease between us, as if there was never any reason to fear us losing what we built together.

"One last thing," he says. "Did you listen to any of my messages?" He realizes my answer before I can respond. "Right. I don't blame you. Detective Vale has issued a DNA seizure warrant for you. To compare to the crime scene and trace found on the victim. I mean, Cameron."

This makes sense. I was at her home. I may have been the last person, besides the killer, to see her alive.

"It's nothing to worry about," Rhys assures. "It will rule you out as a suspect."

"You're still acting as my attorney?"

"If you'll have me."

His response echos a promise far more committed than just acting in my defense. "Then we'll handle that, too, tomorrow."

"All right."

As we settle beneath the covers, the droning of the air-conditioner lulls me into a sense of calm. Rhys's body heat against my side is a comfort.

Still, my subconscious begs to be heard, my mind churning as I will my eyes closed. So for once, I don't bury my voice. As we lie here, Rhys's arm linking me close, I tell him why the first note shamed me into running and never talking about it.

How I believed the sender of that note may have had reason to want me dead. The awful person I was painted to be: the degraded college student who slept with her professor. The scandal lurking right around the corner.

I was the mud.

I admit that I wanted the man to be real—that I wanted to believe he wrote the letter to send me away, to save me again. I know it's a ridiculous theory, childlike and naive, but I needed to believe in...something. Otherwise I was just a scared victim running from her life.

We whisper into the night, sharing our secrets. He tells me about the case he was assigned to before we met, where he suspected an agent manufactured evidence. This led to the bullet he took in the field. Our fears and allegiance to those we loved and trusted kept us from speaking out. Another thing we share.

Secrets are only able to haunt when they stay buried. Like a ghost crossing over into the light, once they're exposed, all that's left is peace.

❧ 28 ❧

YOU

LAKIN: NOW

3:00 a.m. is known as the witching hour. It's said that evil spirits and ghosts are most active and powerful at this time of night. Nearly a couple hundred years ago, the church believed it was due to lack of prayers during this hour.

That's a good theory. The last thing I want to do as I stir awake is pray, my body aching from muscle exertion—both good and bad. But maybe I should. Send some entreaty up into the clouds, seeking an answer.

I've tried everything else to recover the memory of my attack.

Mind too restless to fall back asleep, I ease out of bed, trying not to disturb Rhys.

A light illuminates from the table near the window. A notification on my phone. I set the device to silent, but the light is bright enough to make me alert. As I pad closer, I grab my key ring from my bag.

The USB drive dangles there, a mockery of the story of my life. The memories recorded in my book aren't real. At least, not all of them. This makes me question what else is false.

The recurring dream I experienced leading up to my attack. The one I thought was, somehow, a warning, a premonition. The actual dream most likely never happened. Repressed memories have a way of relocating, transplanting themselves in other areas of the mind.

The truth is, it's far more likely there was never a dream at all. After the trauma I suffered, my mind may have rebuilt the memories, installing bits of the attack into a dreamlike sequence. Distorted glimpses of that night, rearranging the moments before my death in a way I could accept, by remembering the attack as a dream when I tried to recall the event.

I touch my belly, lightly tracing the scar tissue beneath Rhys's shirt.

I should write it all down. Now. While the recovered memories are fresh. I can compare them to the dream to determine what is fact and what is false.

Reaching for the notepad and pen on the table, I knock the curtain aside. A splinter of moonlight dances over the table and my phone. Now fully awake, I pick up the phone and illuminate the screen.

A text message appears: *I'm here. It's time we meet. Come down alone.*

I stare at the message, my heart rate climbing. I glance at Rhys, then back at the screen. The number is unknown. Of course, it is. Most likely a burner.

I push the curtain back and peek out the window. The

rain has stopped, and it's eerily still outside. Then movement catches my eye.

A figure travels through the parking lot.

Dread coils in my stomach as I push the curtain farther aside. The person below stops near the rental sedan and looks up. A tremor of fear skitters down my back as they appear to be looking directly at me. *They can't see me...* But still, I step away.

Meet me.

The words written in the note from yesterday flare to life, as if they've been whispered in my ear.

The devil's hour. It would be decidedly stupid for me to meet this person now, alone. I know this, and yet the urgent press to dart to the parking lot and catch them before they can escape thrums through me.

Who's down there hidden behind the shadows? Who's waiting for me to come?

Rationally, Rhys and I should investigate together. My anxiety is climbing. What if this is my only chance to confront my killer? Cam's killer? What if I can end this before anyone else gets hurt?

Yes, that's what I want—but I'm not a saint.

I whisper the word, and my soul feels as light as air. "*Revenge.*"

Not justice. Not closure.

Retribution.

Right now, feeling the aching void of what was stolen from me anew...that person doesn't get to have justice.

I'm the nexus. This started with me—and it needs to end with me.

The decision was made before I closed the text message. I slip on a pair of jeans and tuck in Rhys's shirt.

His scent envelops me, comforting, lending me his strength. I want to keep him close, even though I have to leave him behind.

I eye his service weapon on the nightstand table.

I've never shot a gun before. It seems likely that the perpetrator could turn it around on me, so I decide against taking the weapon and instead snag the metal handcuffs from his belt.

One last glance behind as Rhys slumbers in bed, then I slip out of the room.

⚜

The air outside the hotel is humid despite the early hour. The mugginess thickens my throat as I hastily maneuver through the parking lot. I weave around cars with purpose toward the sedan. If that person is still out here, if they're watching, waiting, I don't want them to think I'm aware.

I click the key fob, and the sedan's lights blink a couple of times. I wait a moment longer, pretending to check my phone, giving them time to approach me, before I settle behind the wheel.

My heart gallops audibly in my ears.

What am I doing?

I'm crazy.

I look through the windshield, not spotting any notes. Maybe I imagined them, the wires in my brain still crossed, faulty. I breathe a curse and rest my forehead against the wheel.

An engine cranks, light beams into the car's interior.

Slowly, I look up.

For a moment, I'm blinded by the headlights of the car

directly across the lot. Then, as the car backs out of the parking spot, my eyes adjust. I can make out the profile of a woman in the driver's seat. It's the hair; I recognize the long waves. The light shade.

Chelsea.

My mind springs to this conclusion before I can rationalize another logical reason as to why some random woman would be hovering around a car at three in the morning.

The car idles in the parking lot, and pressure beats at my temples.

She's waiting for me.

I key the ignition with a shaky hand and crank the car. Once I'm backed out, the other car—a sleek, black Toyota—pulls ahead, turning right out of the hotel. Steeling my nerves, I follow the car onto the main road.

We coast on the highway like this for an hour, me muttering to myself, scolding myself for my lunacy—which I can only blame the witching hour for my rash choice—when I realize where the woman is leading me.

My head beams illuminate the road sign for Silver Lake.

An oily film coats my stomach. I glance at the passenger seat, at my phone. Steering one-handed, I grab the device and type out a quick but detailed text to Rhys. My thumb hovers over the Send button…

The black car flips on the blinker.

I set the phone on the seat. I leave the message app open, just in case I need Rhys to know. I made a note of the car, the license plate, and a vague description of the woman driving.

Even though I didn't name her specifically, he'll come

to the same conclusion; Chelsea. It was Rhys's theory, after all. Regardless of his reluctance to profile a woman killer, Chelsea had motive.

Piece it together:

My pregnancy stood in the way of her marrying Drew.

The first note was meant to scare me away when I survived the attack.

We will have to find a connection to investigate—but Drew may have known Joanna Delany intimately. Another possible threat to Chelsea, or simple jealousy.

The newest notes: the author didn't want us investigating Joanna's cold case.

Cam's confession, once confirmed, would have revealed that Chelsea was not Drew's alibi, therefore Chelsea is now without one for the night of my attack.

The method in Cam's murder was different; the perpetrator purposely spared her unborn baby. A show of remorse.

Which goes back to: *who pulled me from the lake?* Only a killer, who suffers a conflicting bout of guilt, would rescue their victim. And the evidence states that there was no one else there that night. Just me and my killer.

All the pieces are there…they just have to be linked.

So whatever this woman has to say to me now, I'm ready—I'm ready to face my killer.

Following two car-lengths behind, I make the turn into the Dock House parking lot.

I hang back, my hands gripped to the wheel, as the Toyota parks in the spot nearest the water. My breathing is too loud in the silence of the car. My chest prickles as adrenaline crashes my system.

I go for the band around my wrist, needing the sharp

bite of pain to ground me, and find my wrist bare. "Dammit." Okay. Think. I dip sideways, losing sight of the car for only a few seconds, as I search the glove box.

Rhys is always prepared. For anything. I riffle through the items until I find the roll of coins and tape. As I situate myself in the driver's seat, I eye the car as I grip the roll and wrap my hand with the bandage tape.

The car door swings open, she exits, and I quickly pull my hair back into a low bun, feeding a strand through the knot to hold it in place. If this comes down to a scuffle, I want to at least be prepared to fight. I watch her walk toward the dock. I slip my phone into my back pocket and check the handcuffs I stuffed in my front pocket.

I open the door.

It's been years since I was last here, when Rhys brought me back, and nothing has changed. The Dock House is a wormhole in time. Untouched. String lights canopy the outside deck. A makeshift tiki hut stands center, sporting a wraparound bar. A plank stage two feet off the deck floor makes up the backside, where bands play live music. The same jukebox still separates the outside bar from the inside seating area.

Nausea engulfs my senses, and I fight down the bile trying to choke me. Last time, I was stronger. Last time, I had Rhys by my side. I wasn't facing this dread alone.

I'm seconds away from giving in to the fear when I spot her on the pier. Hands tucked into a gray trench coat, her back to me, she looks out over the lake, her countenance just as serene as the still water.

My blood ignites.

This woman who has taken so much from me…

I let the anger take root, chasing back the tremors of

fear. Gripping the coin roll in a tight fist, I head toward her, not softening my footfalls. I stop in the middle of the dock, inhale a fortifying breath.

I've stepped into my dream.

"I'm here."

She doesn't move. As I study her profile, my brows knit together. This woman is taller than Chelsea, and something seems…off.

She removes a hand from her pocket and tugs off her hair. The blond wig drops to the wooden planks.

My heart seizes inside my chest cavity. Before the realization is confirmed, the cruel veracity is already hitting.

And when they turn around, the world shifts.

"You."

29

BODY OF WATER

LAKIN: NOW AND THEN

Andrew Abbot was the most beautiful man I'd ever seen.

He was intelligent. Refined. Passionate.

He was a teacher of the mind, but also my first lesson in life and love.

And he *saw* me.

When he looked at me that first day in his lecture hall, all the world and its melancholy fell away, and I was *seen*.

Drew stands at the end of the pier now, so altered from the man that was the sun I used to orbit around. What I see is the truth that my young and vulnerable self couldn't discern back then. The selfish, narcissistic manipulator that used people for his own gratification as he maneuvered them like puppets.

He removes the coat. Drops it next to the wig. "Was she followed?"

My brows draw together in confusion, my mouth

parting to ask a question, until I'm silenced by the cold touch of a blade to my back.

"No," Torrance says. I recognize his deep voice. I hold still as his large hands skim my body, patting me down. He chuckles at the bandage wrapping my hand for self-defense, then removes my phone from my back pocket. My eyes seal closed.

I hear the phone hit the dock, and the resounding *crunch* as Torrance smashes it beneath his foot. Making me untraceable. "And she won't be," he confirms.

Torrance nudges my shoulders roughly, forcing me to walk up the dock.

So many theories… I had so many on my murder board. But never, not once, did this scenario present. "How?" I ask this of Drew, gaze trained hard on him. "The both of you?"

Drew crosses his arms over his broad chest. "I want to be here just about as much as you do," he answers me.

Torrance tugs me to a stop. "Oh, come on now. Life is all about the memories. Reliving our most important experiences. This was a defining one right here. For the both of you."

I shake my head, clutch the coin roll bound in my hand. I whip around to face Torrance. "Did you kill me, or save me?" I demand. "Did you pull me from the lake for some kind of twisted game? I want answers!"

"Save you?" Torrance tilts his head, his eyes too open, too intense. I back up a step. "Tell her what she wants to know, Andrew. Every victim should have a final request."

A shiver slithers over my skin, and I sneak a glance at the car. Then out over the lake. At the white lotuses bathed in moonlight. The water too still. That grave of tangled stalks waiting, beckoning me home.

No.

Fight.

The hollow footsteps rebound off the dock, the water a perfect conductor to send an electric jolt of awareness through me as Drew closes in. I turn so that I'm between them, trapped. "Why?" It leaves my mouth as a whispered plea.

"You made this happen," Drew says, disgust evident on his shadowed face. "You were always so jealous of Chelsea, fearful of her stealing me away. You manifested your own fear. And when it came true, you did the most unoriginal thing." He scoffs. "Got knocked up. To keep us together. To trap me. To ruin me. I couldn't allow that to happen."

Still the psych professor. Still trying to *teach* me about myself. I look down, stare at the dark water lapping between the slats.

A flash of my dream. A glimpse into the past. My vision tunnels as his words generate a sensation, an image. Fear encases me as the sharp slash of a razor-sharp blade tears into my flesh. Red stains my skin.

I blink the memory away, trying to stay in the present. "You attacked me," I say. "Right here. On the dock." I touch my unbandaged hand to my stomach, the pain alive and real.

Drew's beautiful face draws together in anger. "You forced me, Cynthia. You wouldn't listen to reason when it came to—" He breaks off, turns his head away. "My intent wasn't to end your life."

But my death was the result, and he felt no remorse.

The way he feels none now.

I sense Torrance moving closer. "It was astonishing," he says. "See, when Cam changed her mind and didn't follow me home, I remembered you were here. I came back." He pulls my hair loose of the bun, strokes the strands. "I'd never witnessed anything so passionate. I was in awe. All my life, I felt this hollow, empty void. This lack of emotion that I hid from the world. Nothing made me feel...until I saw the beautiful, violent dance between you and Drew."

I cringe away from his touch. "You hide well."

"It's a learned skill."

All my training, all Rhys's training, and we both missed the clues. Torrance is a psychopath. Lack of empathy did more than allow him to watch my brutal murder; it fostered something dark and deviant inside him. Ignited a sick desire.

Torrance wouldn't rescue me from the lake. He's not built that way. "You left me to drown," I say, piecing the night together. "Then what? You went home and jerked off?"

His laugh is callous. "Well, yes. But first I cleaned up the scene. I understood enough to know that Drew's crime was one of passion. He left behind the murder weapon"— he prods the tip of the knife between my shoulder blades —"so I hosed down the dock. I made sure my source, should I ever need anything in the future, would be safe."

That's why there was no DNA or any evidence to test, and how Drew made it back in time to be with Cam. "Why did you do it?"

"To torment me," Drew answers. He pulls out a crumpled wad of letters.

"Blackmail?" I ask, appalled. It seems so petty, to have suffered these years for something so inconsequential as money.

"No." Torrance steps forward, his shadow looming in the moonlight. Those shallow, dark pools stare right through me. "He had answers. I wanted to know what he felt when he first thrust the knife into your belly. Gutting you like a fish. And when that wasn't enough, stabbed and raked the blade over your chest, mutilating someone that he once loved."

Ripping the letters in half, Drew shreds them into small pieces, then tosses them into the lake. Torrance sent the note to me, I realize. He'd been playing some twisted game, stalking both killer and victim.

"Are we done yet?" Drew says. "Let's get this over with."

My gaze flits between the men. Adrenaline mounting. I take a step away, and Torrance raises the knife.

"Patience," he says, watching the moonlight glint across the weapon. "You know, I tried not to be this way. I resisted the urges. I relived that moment in my mind, never acting on it. Until Agent Nolan showed up. His probing questions ignited that spark all over again…and I just had to know what it felt like for myself. I thought Jo would be perfect, then I waited for the right moment. Once I was confident I could pull it off, I finally did it." His handsome features mutate into a lethal scowl. "But it was lacking. It wasn't even close to that first time."

Fear still clawing internally, I lift my chin in a show of bravado. Now this, I understand. "You experienced a first kill vicariously. As a voyeur. A killer never gets that first experience back. It's a never-ending chase for a high, like a drug addict."

A haunted void fills his dark gaze. "Jo was supposed to be perfect. I memorized everything... But do you know how hard it is to actually replicate a murder? TV makes copycat killings look so easy. It's not. Fighting the victim... wounds inflicted in the wrong places. It's fucking hard."

I swallow, sending the acrid taste of bile into my bowels. He killed Joanna. So senselessly. He tried to replicate Drew's attack...his murder...and he's flippantly comparing the act to television. His voice is passive. Unaffected. His act of violence an afterthought.

I glance between them, pulse slamming my arteries. I have to keep them talking, find a way out. "Which one of you killed Cam?"

"I tried again," Torrance admits. "But her body—" He shakes his head. "She wasn't right. The baby was too far along. Drew kept whining."

My gaze snaps to him. He was a part of her violent end. He helped take her life, take her away from her child and family. "You're weak. Pathetic," I say. "A disgusting narcissist."

"It was a necessity," Drew says. "She could implicate me. She had to know if she ever said anything... She shouldn't have met with you. But I made sure her baby would be all right. I called 9-1-1 from her house."

Filmy acid roils my stomach. How can he justify taking Cam's life? The same way he justified killing me?

"And we needed to practice." Torrance circles me, and dread flares in my veins. "So we could get it right this time."

"You lured me here."

"For a reenactment," Torrance confirms. "It's what's missing. We need an ending."

Fear cramps my muscles, every fiber of my being screaming to *run*.

Torrance holds out the hilt of the knife in Drew's direction. "The knife I used to cut Cam's limes that night. Ironic, isn't it? That Andrew here would choose this one from the bar."

"What's to stop me from using it on you?" Drew asks.

Torrance scowls. "Because you want the investigation to go away. You want your victim to stop dredging up the past. So that you and your wife can live your cozy little, white picket-fence life. So that you can finally be free."

"You'll never be free of this, Drew," I say. "My partner will piece it together. Agent Nolan won't stop until he proves it was you and you're locked away. Freedom gone."

Drew accepts the weapon. "Like hell I won't be free."

Everything happens fast then. I try to dart past Torrance. His long arms surround me. He grabs my waist and hauls me around to face Drew. He locks my arms behind my head, holding me in place.

"This way," Torrance says, breathless, "I get the perfect view."

I struggle against his hold, my feet kicking out at Drew. I can feel Torrance's excitement against my back as Drew raises the knife.

"In a way, we're doing this for you, Cynthia." Torrance locks his arms tighter, an iron-clad grip. "Do you really want to live in a world where every single person in your life betrayed you? Do you want to keep running? What kind of life is that?"

My chest engulfs in flames, my breaths sawing my lungs like the sharp blade in Drew's hand. He's watching me, marking his moment to strike. "Don't, Drew. You don't have to do this. Not like last time…"

Time folds. I tunnel through a wave. A moonless night. Blackness all around. The crickets and frogs. Drew on the dock. Coming toward me. A rising bubble of hope that he'd come to talk, to work things out…before I see the hatred marring his handsome features. Then the blood-stained lotus in the water…

As I blink into the present, a serene calm washes over me. "Who planted the lotuses at Joanna's crime scene?"

This stops Drew's advance. "What?"

Torrance forces me forward. "She's stalling. Do it, Andrew. Finish what you started."

I close my eyes. I don't believe in the supernatural. I don't believe in premonitions or ghosts, or victims reaching out from beyond the grave. We can spend our whole life searching for meaning, for a sign, and in the end, the only answer to life is to live.

During our partnership, Rhys made sure I knew more than the basics of self-defense. He never considered me a victim, and he made sure I'd never be one again.

Drew arcs the knife in the air and bites his lip in concentration. He thrusts the blade into my stomach, and pain lights up my nervous system. A scream wrenched from the bottom of my lungs imbues the early morning air. As the weapon is yanked free, Torrance covers my mouth.

"Again!" Torrance shouts.

The silver blade glistens with my blood. I try to latch

on to a thought—a plan. In his attempt to silence me, Torrance freed my arm. I grip the coin roll and, mustering every ounce of strength, I throw my body into the swing and strike his face.

He curses. The distraction is enough to free myself. I wriggle loose of his arms and fall to the dock. Vomit claws up my throat, the piercing pain in my abdomen beginning to throb. My heart pulses in my ears, my vision wavers.

No. I've been through worse. I've survived worse.

Drew doesn't hesitate; he barrels toward me. I manage to roll out of his reach. The knife strikes the dock, the blade wedged between the planks. Just enough time...I wrestle the handcuffs from my pocket.

Torrance didn't think they were a weapon. Something to laugh off like the wrapped coin roll. I use them now. I clutch my fingers around the curved steel and make a fist, then aim for Drew's face. My knuckles blaze with the force of impact.

"Oh my, God." I breathe through the pain as I click the cuffs open.

Drew holds his face, covering the red gash on his cheek. "You bitch."

From my peripheral, I see Torrance coming my way. As he goes for my legs, I let him seize me, drag me backward. Then I rear up and latch one cuff around his wrist.

The sky is becoming a gray-blue backdrop as morning peaks against the horizon.

With the breaking light, I fight against Drew as he dives on top of me. He forces my back to the dock. Torrance mounts my shoulders. Drew's hands slide around my neck, and a blind moment of panic snares me as I realize—if I let this happen—they'll finally kill me.

I secure the other cuff to Drew's wrist, locking him and Torrance together.

In the distance, a siren sounds. The noise cracks against the morning, a splintering echo from my dream.

"Fuck." Torrance releases my shoulders and yanks against the handcuff.

Drew fights back, dragging his accomplice across the dock. They both lunge for the knife.

I use the forgotten moment to inch backward. I scuttle away from the carnage, a red slash of blood in my wake as I escape.

I watch Drew punch Torrance, and Torrance retaliate with an elbow to Drew's nose. Blood spurts against the gray sky. But it's Torrance who retrieves the knife. Fear petrifies my limbs and I stop, frozen. Trying to be unseen. But Torrance doesn't advance on me.

Horror webs through me as Torrance slashes the knife downward—again and again—severing Drew's hand at the wrist. Drew releases a primal wail that rends the air. Torrance kicks away from Drew, and the bloody, severed hand.

I'm cold, my blood drained, as Torrance stands and walks toward me, knife held at his thigh.

He stands over me. And I know this is the end. All the fight evaporates, and I suddenly become accepting. I love Rhys. I got to be with him once and to finally understand what it means to be truly loved in return. I found my answers. I can let go.

The *whoop whoop* of a police siren smashes through the hollow morning, compelling Torrance to look up. He must decide that my demise isn't worth what precious time he might have left to escape.

"Maybe next time," he says, sending the blade into my arm.

A flesh wound. A taunt.

Torrance flees the pier, leaving me behind.

It's over.

I rip the bandage of coins from my hand and toss it aside.

I lay my head back against the wooden planks of the dock. I let the pain grow and ebb as the lake laps against the posts.

I breathe and stare at the sky, watching the dark clouds roll across, and then he's towering from above.

"You slutty, little bitch. You don't get to take everything from me."

Drew descends on me, tearing the knife from my flesh with his good hand. I raise my arms to block his attack as he slashes, splitting my skin, my arms becoming bathed in dark-red.

I try to claw at his face, but I'm fighting blind as blood leaks into my eyes. Then the bite of cold water stings my body.

We fall into the lake. The murky water swallows me.

30

THAT NIGHT

LAKIN: THEN

I'm seated at the end of the dock, my feet dangling over the edge. I thought about laying down right there, just giving up, forgetting about Drew and Chelsea and the baby…

I wanted the silent night to swallow me.

Footsteps sounded on the dock. A slow, hollow *thud* against the planks.

I quickly got to my feet and turned, recognition slamming into me full force.

"Drew?"

Elation fluttered in my chest, until I remembered the last thing he said to me during our fight.

Should've never fucked you.

I swallowed the ache as he slowly approached. "Why are you here?"

"Do you know how embarrassing it is to have the cops escort you home?"

"Drew…" My eyes closed for a brief moment. "I'm tired. I'm just too tired to do this again." I stuffed my hands into my hoodie pockets and started toward the other side.

I made it a few feet from him, deciding to hurriedly sidestep, when I glimpsed the knife in his hand. Shock snatched my breath. Ice-cold fear prickled my skin.

"We're not done yet," he said. His breath wreaked of alcohol. He tapped the flat of the blade against his jean-clad thigh. "What do you plan to do about the baby, Cynthia?"

I stepped backward. I'd never feared Drew…not in this sense. But there was something off in his voice. He wasn't himself, the way he kept tapping the knife. Even when we were shouting in each other's faces, a glass vase thrown against the wall. Shards spraying, fists hitting walls… I didn't fear he'd physically harm me.

"Stop, Drew. You're drunk."

"We can be together," he said, ignoring me, advancing. Knife tapping. "I just can't have a baby ruin my life."

I shook my head slowly. "So, you want me to get rid of it and then we'll live happily ever after?"

"It makes more sense than trying to raise a child no one wants, doesn't it?"

"And what about Chelsea?"

"She's nothing to me."

"I saw you. The way you looked at her…" I tried to force the image away, the memory still painful. Me walking up to his door. Her answering. Them *together*. I went to tell Drew about the baby, and instead I came face-to-face with my nightmare. "How could you make me feel like I was the crazy one? Like I was imagining things?"

"So you won't get rid of it?"

I felt as if I'd been slapped. "No, Drew. I'm not just getting rid of it. This is my body. My choice." Anger surging, I forgot the knife as stormed forward, needing to escape.

Drew blocked me. "I'm not much for philosophy, but Wittgenstein was pretty brilliant when he said: Whereof one cannot speak, thereof one must be silent."

Confusion twisted inside me, and then a terrifying reality shattered my world as Drew planted the knife in my belly.

31

OF PAST AND PRESENT

LAKIN: NOW

The memory bursts. Cold water tunnels down my throat as I release a muffled scream beneath the black water. Thick stalks tangle my arms, my hands moving too slowly through the water to clear a path.

A sudden, sharp pain brings me back. Drew lances my side with the knife again. And I'm awake. The dream-like trance forgotten as I claw at his arm underwater, desperate for air.

Blood clouds the water, obscuring my vision further. I feel the blade swipe my shoulder, and I grab hold of Drew's forearm. Our eyes lock. Through the murky lake water and the red haze of our mingled blood, I sense our bodies sinking.

He attempts to thrust the knife at my chest, but I have both hands anchored to his arm, the struggle twisting us farther down into the lotus stems. I kick out and plant my foot against his stomach. He tries to use his other arm to dislodge me—but he's without a hand, the wound too new and shocking for him to use to his advantage.

His face twists in rage, and finally he drops the knife. I watch it drift down, becoming lost, before the severe grip around my throat steals my senses. Panic flares, and I gulp down lake water in an effort to scream, my temples pulsing with pressure as my vision darkens.

Teeth gritted, Drew clamps my throat, squeezing my windpipe. I latch on to his hand, my fingernails digging into his skin, as I rake for freedom. Then Drew presses his lips to mine, stealing the last of my breath. The kiss of death.

I'm submerged beneath the overpowering fear of it.

I've died before.

I can feel death's oily tentacles winding around my body.

My feet touch the bottom of the lake. And just as my eyes close, a cold and calm peace settling over me, Drew releases my neck. He kicks off the floor, his body propelled upward.

I'm not dying.

I grab hold of the lotus stalk snarling my arm and loop it around his leg. Halted, Drew panics, bubbles frothing from his open mouth. My chest burns with the need for air as I watch Drew struggle uselessly against the lotuses.

I remember...the feel of the coarse stalks tugging at my hair. My hands frantically searching for a way out of the underwater maze of vines and darkness.

I begin to drift upward, my gaze latched on to Drew's fight at the bottom of the lake, as he sucks in water, trapped in the wiry grave. I don't look away. I keep watching until his movements stop.

Every wound makes itself known as the adrenaline ebbs. I've been stabbed. Strangled. Lack of oxygen caves my chest. I've lost sight of Drew, the darkness becoming complete. I desperately kick my feet and peddle to reach the top, but my discombobulated state has lost the way to the surface.

The clotting dark consumes me. I recall the moment I decided to die nearly four years ago, accepting my place among the lotuses…then the fight as I refused to surrender. The memory surrounds me; pervading the lake and opening up a window into the past.

My body was numb of any pain. My condition too far gone. I felt nothing but the water in my lungs and the lotus stems leaching life from my body. Fight or flight was all I knew. I clawed my way through the web of vines until I reached the surface. I floated there, blood emptying from my veins, the black night shrouding me in an abyss.

Until I heard the frogs and crickets, and I realized I was nearing the shore. A second, last wind to save myself…and I dragged my body through the vegetation. I only rested once I felt earth beneath my feet. I let my body wash up onto the shore.

I'm floating somewhere between the bottom and the surface of the lake now, lost in that tranquility of acceptance. I don't have to fear, to hide, anymore. I'm resigned to let go…

The shimmering waves appear.

They flicker above me in a crown of light.

The moon, rippling on the water surface, showing me the way.

I reach, and reach, my muscles on fire, my lungs

concaved. Pain is good. It means I'm alive. I hold on to this hope as I fight to gain an inch toward the surface.

It's too far away...

A silhouette of a man materializes amid the halo of light.

Past and present collide. Time suspends, folding in on itself, like the leaf of a lotus as it touches at the seams. I'm frightened of my mind. Terrified of what I know is happening. How many neurons fire at the moment of death? Have I been trapped inside a Jacob's Ladder, my death stretched out endlessly, living and dying in a loop?

Blackness dims my sight around the edges, my vision tunnels. All I see is *him*.

A hand crashes through the water surface. He touches me. I *feel* him. He's real. He drags me to the surface. The flashlight in his hand is forgotten, the halo of light drifting past me, as he hauls me over the edge of a boat.

"I've got you."

Rhys's voice is ethereal and home all at once. He's the fusion between then and now—illusion and reality. He's always been with me.

"She's not breathing," he says. I don't know who he's talking to.

I'm not breathing.

His mouth touches mine. His hands pump my chest. Air blasts my airway over and over.

I purge water from my lungs in a violent cough. My own voice touches my ears, and I'm shaken, but alive. I blink several times until his face becomes clear.

"Lakin..." He says my name like a question, his voice a shiver against the morning.

"I'm here," I say.

His arms surround me, he pulls me to his chest. We hold onto each other.

Daybreak crests the sky, the fragile light revealing I'm not that far from shore. Men in uniform are in the fishing boat with us. I remember the sirens I heard on the dock.

"How?" I ask.

He brushes my wet hair from my face as he inspects me, not content until he's searched every inch of my body. "You're bleeding."

"I was stabbed."

"Hand me the emergency kit," he demands. He peels my soaked clothes from my body as gently as possible. The pain is starting to resurface. "Stomach wound."

I let him bandage my stomach and arm, and as the local police steer us toward the shore, Rhys applies pressure to my stomach. A person can suffer a gut wound for days; but I'm scared to ask how bad it is; I don't want to shatter the hope of this moment.

"I tracked your phone to the last pinged location," Rhys finally answers. "I'd have come here anyway if I couldn't do a trace. Detective Dutton responded."

I glance over. The old detective from my case is in the boat with us.

"It was you," I say to Rhys.

"What are you talking about?" He's looking ahead, destination in sight. He's fighting to get me to a hospital. "Radio the EMT truck," he orders the cop at the helm. "Have them ready."

"You're him," I say, my voice strained. "You rescued me from the lake."

Rhys looks down, into my eyes. Awareness crashes

through him. He presses his lips to my forehead, a kiss so tender it aches through me.

As we dock, I hear the search, flashlights slash the dawn, as uniforms hunt for the unknown assailant who evaded arrest.

Rhys carries me to the ambulance and demands to ride with me to Silver Lake Memorial. He grasps my hand, not letting go, even as the EMT covers my mouth and nose with an oxygen mask and dresses the stab wound.

His hand pulses mine. "You rescued yourself," he says. "But I'll be the man of your dreams, Lakin. I can be him."

I let the dark press of sleep claim me then. Holding on to Rhys. Holding on to the hope of us.

EPILOGUE

W e are all connected. Through time and space, atoms and neurons. Villains and heroes. We're all linked in a cosmic web, fighting to live. Fighting for truth.

The last words of the book. The End.

A lethargic purge, the truest crime story I've ever penned. The one I lived through. The story of two women and their crimes solved together. The title of the manuscript for *In Her Wake* proved to be a genuine representation of our story. I was in Joanna's wake. Her murder led me to our killers.

Once I completed the book, I sent an early proof copy to Ms. Delany for approval—to make sure my story would not detract from Joanna's, and that I had honored her daughter's memory properly. Our book is slated to release to the world next year.

I thanked Bethany Delany in the acknowledgments for more than just her participation; her maternal instinct pointed us to Mike Rixon. Our first lead.

During his questioning, Mike admitted to local

authorities that he had always harbored a fear about his half-brother, about what he was. A social media post captured him saying: "At times, I wondered if there was something wrong with him, something off. I had my suspicions, but I wasn't sure."

Mike saw the way Torrance looked at Joanna—that's why Mike was protective over her at the Tiki Hive. What Bethany had noticed during her visit one evening to the restaurant before her daughter was discovered in a lake.

When Rhys and I showed up at the Tiki Hive to question Mike, he could've revealed his suspicions then. But he was also quoted saying: "He's still family."

I suppose that's the reason why Mike didn't correct Torrance when he pointed us toward Kohen. Mike wasn't charged with hindering an investigation, however. Suspicion doesn't equate to factual knowledge of a crime.

No, the evidence was there this time. Torrance, under pressure from the FBI's investigation, made mistakes during Cam's murder. Dr. Keller, the medical examiner, found trace DNA on the dress Cam was wearing at the time.

I recall how Torrance claimed he and Drew had "practiced" on Cam. How Torrance had held my arms behind my head, his excitement pressed hard against my back. The dark spark that was planted in him all those years ago, aroused by my murder, was what told the story of his involvement.

I'm glad that, even if events hadn't unfolded as they did, Cam would've been the one to close the cases—that she'd avenge her death in the end.

Detective Vale made the match to the pre-ejaculate on Cam's dress to Torrance.

There is no such thing as a perfect murder.

Torrance Carver was apprehended at the Dock House the morning of his and Drew's attack on me. While I was being rushed to Silver Lake Memorial, Detective Dutton and the Leesburg PD discovered Torrance hiding in the kitchen cooler of the Dock House.

It's far less dramatic than I imagined for his ending.

But it's realistic, and now Torrance is incarcerated and awaiting trial, to be judged by a jury. With definitive proof of his crimes, Rhys and I are sure the state of Florida will get the maximum for his sentence.

As for Drew, one bit of evidence was able to tie him to the crimes. The picture the ME took of my scars. Dr. Keller matched those images to the other murders. Same murder weapon. Drew had carelessly dropped the knife in the lake, and Torrance had retrieved it. Using the same weapon to brutally murder Joanna Delany, to replicate the first murder he witnessed.

Then, of course, there was my statement.

Andrew Abbot was dredged from the lake, pronounced dead at Silver Lake Memorial…just a few rooms down from where I was being operated on.

When I think about Drew, I don't envision him on a gurney, or in a casket. I see him floating in dark water, lotus stalks encasing his body.

An eerie role reversal for victim and killer. Instead of me—my death—at the bottom of the lake, my killer found his fate. It's the kind of macabre irony that leaves me feeling numb.

Even now, I'm not entirely sure how I feel about Drew. What he stole from me. The level of vindictive selfishness that turned a college professor into a killer.

But I have come to a point of acceptance. I had thought that, when I left Silver Lake the first time, I was saving myself, starting over. I believed I had accepted my circumstances—that I could endeavor to be like the leaves of the lotus and cleanse myself of the filth from my past.

The truth is, I was trapped. It might have been Drew that put me in the lake, and Torrance's pathology played a part, but it was my fear, my shame, that kept me at the bottom.

The lies we tell ourselves are the hardest to see.

Although Rhys always suspected Drew of my attempted murder, there was never any hard evidence. The timeline didn't match up, and the circumstantial evidence wasn't strong enough. When people deem to keep secrets, the truth is difficult to uncover. That is, until one peg is jarred loose.

All it takes is one person to speak out, and the house of lies crumbles.

Cam's admission may have come too late for her, but by finally admitting the truth, all the other puzzle pieces started to align.

I did attend her funeral. I did meet her husband and their infant baby girl. Her name is Calliope.

Every person played a part in my crime. Whether they were an active participant, or simply selfish, or passive, like Chelsea, who is now a victim in her own right, left behind to carry the weight of Drew's shameful legacy.

Every person from my past did, somehow, play a part —and if they were judged deserving of a punishment from a higher power, they've now answered for their sins.

The murder board has been erased. The book is finished.

Newest case file in hand, I pad to where Rhys is transcribing an interview. His laptop rests on his lap as he pecks at the keyboard, his socked feet propped on the table.

I sit beside him and open the file. After my case was closed, Rhys wondered if I was done with my hunt for justice within the cold case division. And I'll be honest, I did take a moment of pause. I could go back to school, complete my degree. Become a psychologist.

My answer to him: I reached into my box of files and plucked out the Lowenstein case.

Rhys's response: the rare gift of his smile that I savor just for myself.

Soon after we took on the case, I left Missouri, which wasn't too difficult a choice. I had never created a life for myself there. So I packed Lilly and my belongings and flew to Arlington to be with the man who pulled me from the water.

Rhys is my home.

He halts typing mid-sentence and removes his earbuds, a serious expression etching his face. "Did you throw it away?"

I inhale a deep breath, nod. "Didn't even open it."

"All right." He grasps my hand, laces our fingers together. His thumb traces my wrist, free of the band. "Good. You want to read the husband's interview so far?"

Just like that, we move forward.

A letter came in the mail today. It had traveled around the country, bouncing from mailboxes, until it finally found its destination. It was addressed from a Florida correctional penitentiary. From Torrance. A part of me—that part that still ceases to breathe when the memory of that night stirs—wanted to tear the letter open. To read the words and torture myself with trepidation.

We are human. We are flawed. We gravitate to the worst possible outcome because we are designed to expect this, to anticipate the bottom falling out.

Knowledge dispels fear.

Since uncovering the mystery of my fear, I have slain my demons. Whenever doubt creeps into my thoughts, all I have to do is remind myself of this.

So instead, I placed the letter on the kitchen counter and made Rhys aware. He's a part of my story. We face these challenges together.

Victims do not have to suffer alone.

Victims do not have to be victims.

I am a survivor.

I escaped death not once but twice. The first time the Grim Reaper touched my life, I left myself buried in a grave of lotuses. I clung to that death, I ran, afraid of a faceless killer.

Drew did kill me that night—not for just those sixty-seven seconds—he ended my life…because I allowed him to, because I was too ashamed to live. When I finally returned home to my parents, I ultimately learned that, in order to conquer my fear, I had to accept all of my choices, all of my hurt.

We cannot carve our lives into sections. The good and the bad, the beautiful and the ugly moments; one cannot exist without the other. This is the design.

I am not like the leaves of the lotus; I am its petals. Soft and pliable, but also sharp and deadly, like the blade that carved my body. I do not suffer my scars. They're a testament of my strength and will to survive.

I am not unsoiled—but I am not the mud.

I'm free of the mud that held me bound at the bottom for so long.

People much wiser than I have studied and praised the lotus, have written proverbs and songs dedicated to its remarkability. I can only testify as to how it has affected my life.

Buddha may disagree, but for me, the lotus effect represents more than a mere second chance. It's a chance to relive a moment in time; a chance to correct the imbalance.

After I was released from the hospital, Rhys asked me —only once—about what I confessed on the boat.

Was it a premonition? At my moment of death, was I given a glimpse of the future? Did time and space bend and touch at two profound moments of my life?

I don't know the answer. I have no explanation. All I know is that, to only rely on logical explanations can be a desolate existence. If the most intelligent minds in the world knew with absolute surety that there was no other reason beyond what we can see and touch, they would not have devoted their life to the study of time; the quest to explore beyond our tangible reach.

All I know for certain is that we are all searching.

I was searching.

And this time around, I found hope was not a curse.

Rhys and I... We are the beauty that grew out of the mud.

Thank you, lovely reader, for diving deep with Lakin on her journey. If you've made it this far, I hope you'll continue down the rabbit hole with me a bit further with my next psychological thriller *Cruel: A Necrosis of the Mind*.

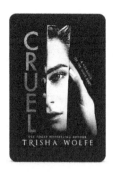

I was born a psychopath. But he made me a killer.

Blakely and Alex collide on a path of immeasurable ruin. A quest to avenge a loved one sparks a dark and deadly obsession, where a dangerous union of cruel minds raises the question: *How far is too far?*

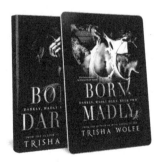

Criminal psychologist London Noble falls for her serial killer patient and enters a dangerous game of cat and mouse. Don't miss this psychologically thrilling romance.

Darkly, Madly Duet

Born, Darkly

Born, Madly

A Necrosis of the Mind Duet

Cruel

Malady

Broken Bonds Series

With Visions of Red

With Ties that Bind

Derision

Standalone Novels

Cellar Door

Lotus Effect

Five of Cups

Living Heartwood Novels

The Darkest Part

Losing Track

Fading Out

ABOUT THE AUTHOR

From an early age, USA Today best-selling author Trisha Wolfe dreamed up imaginary worlds and characters and was accused of talking to herself. Today, she lives in South Carolina with her family and writes full time, using her imaginary worlds as an excuse to continue talking to herself.

Get updates on future releases at TrishaWolfe.com

Want to be the first to hear about new book releases, special promotions, and sale events for all Trisha Wolfe books? Sign up for Trish'a VIP list on her website.

ACKNOWLEDGMENTS

Thank you to:

My amazingly talented critique partner and friend, P.T. Michelle, for reading so quickly, giving me much needed pep talks and advice, wonderful notes, and for your friendship.

My super human beta readers, who read on the fly and offer so much encouragement. I could not write books without your brilliance. Honestly, you are my girls! Melissa & Michell (My M&M's), and Debbie Higgins for reading quickly to give me helpful insight as always.

To the amazing gals in The Lair! I adore you so hard. You keep me sane, where it's perfectly acceptable to be anything but ;) Thank you for all that you do for me, my books. Thank you, girls.

To all the authors out there who share and give shouts outs. You know who you are, and you are amazing.

To my family. My son, Blue, who is my inspiration, thank you for being you. I love you. And my husband, Daniel (my turtle), for your support and owning your title as "the husband" at every book event. To my parents, Debbie and Al, for the emotional support, chocolate, and unconditional love.

Najla Qamber of Najla Qamber Designs, thank you so much for not just creating stunning, take-my-breath-away covers, but for also rocking so hard! You are so much fun to worth with; you take the stress right out of the very stressful task of series cover creation, and I always look forward to working with you on the next project.

There are many, oh, so many people who I have to thank, who have been right beside me during this journey, and who will continue to be there, but I know I can't thank everyone here, the list would go on and on! So just know that I love you dearly. You know who you are, and I wouldn't be here without your support. Thank you so much.

To my readers, you have no idea how much I value and love each and every one of you. If it wasn't for you, none of this could be possible. As cliché as that sounds, I mean it from the bottom of my black heart; I adore you, and hope to always publish books that make you feel.

I owe everything to God, thank you for *everything*.